SERAFINA CROLLA is a wife
who lives between Edinbur
province of Frosinone in It
foothills of the Abruzzi mountains, the daughter of a
shepherd, she has lived an unusual life.

By the same author:

The Wee Italian Girl (Luath Press, 2022)
Domenica (Luath Press, 2022)

Children of This Land

SERAFINA CROLLA

Luath Press Limited

EDINBURGH

www.luath.co.uk

This is a work of fiction; any similarities to any person alive or dead are coincidental.

First published 2023

ISBN: 978-1-80425-108-9

Printed and bound by
Robertson Printers, Forfar

Typeset in 12 point Sabon by
Main Point Books, Edinburgh

In memory of my beloved brother Vincenzo,
who fought bravely against COVID-19
but lost his life.

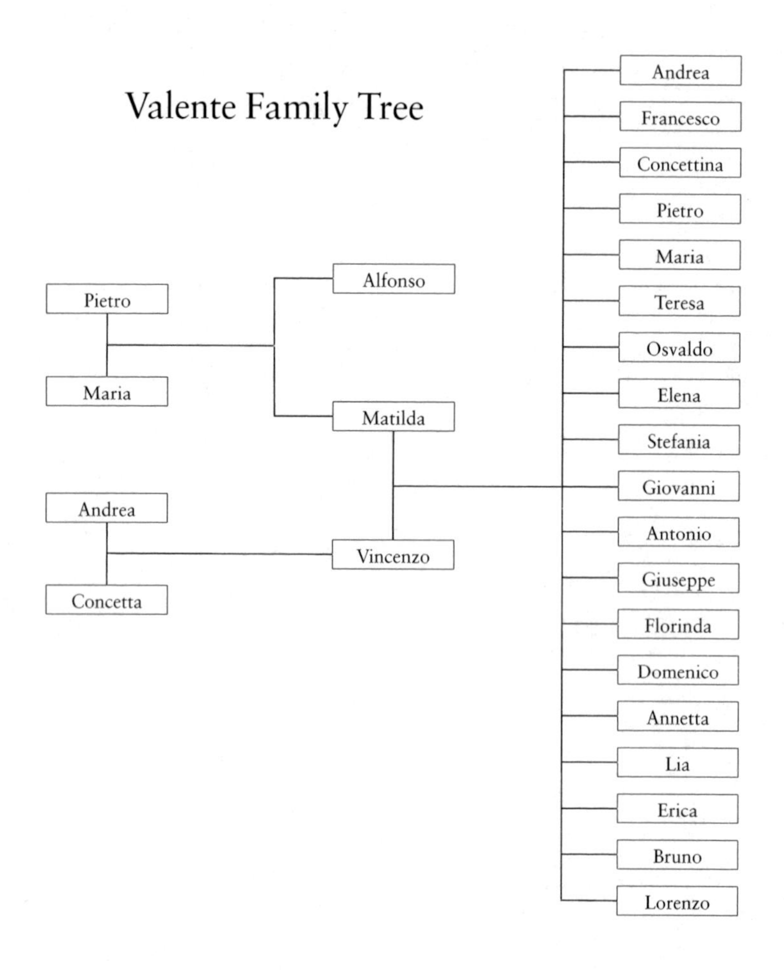
Valente Family Tree
Pietro
Maria
Andrea
Concetta
Alfonso
Matilda
Vincenzo
Andrea
Francesco
Concettina
Pietro
Maria
Teresa
Osvaldo
Elena
Stefania
Giovanni
Antonio
Giuseppe
Florinda
Domenico
Annetta
Lia
Erica
Bruno
Lorenzo

Foreword

CLOSING HER TRILOGY on her native country with *Children of This Land*, Serafina Crolla reconfirms herself as a talented writer and storyteller, shaped by Italian and English matrices.

Taking her cue from one real fact, the epitaph on the tomb of a mother of nineteen children, she imagines the lives of the Valente family in a series of stories set in the 1950s and grounded in the realities of life in our territory, Val Comino, in the aftermath of war.

Among the many vicissitudes of her unfolding tale, the conflict between the long-established customs of rural families and the rapidly altering socio-economic conditions brought by the mid-1900s comes into sharp relief. The Valentes' lives offer few resources, sustenance comes only with hard manual labour and poverty is a recurring threat, and yet the times are bringing new fashions, innovations and an individual dilemma that threatens to tear families apart: should they leave or stay?

Within the struggles of the Valente family, we find the whole condition of life of these times writ small: the ways of thinking, the old and new customs, the rhythm of everyday life and the interruptions of unforeseen events, positive and negative. We find the circumstances that prompted some to emigrate, prevented others from doing so, and made others still choose to stay.

Serafina brings us intimately into the experiences and aspirations, the thoughts and feelings, of both the younger family members and those of the adults who support them with a narrative freshness that captures the nuances of each, profoundly drawing out their individual psychologies. Her humanity closes the gap between past and present with characters that move us, have fun and leave us to reflect on the meaning of life's many events, the wisdom of knowing how to live even in the midst of tough choices.

This book is a treasure trove of special moments brought to life by dialogues painted with objectivity and honesty. Serafina makes us become attached to each character, each co-protagonist, arousing empathy and sympathy in these many intersecting lives and creating an interest in their various situations, trades, decisions and hidden desires which stays with the reader until the end – this is what makes Serafina a great storyteller.

Now we can only wait for the next novel that her fervent creativity will give us – perhaps one that takes us into the mists of Great Britain.

Maria Antonietta Rea, author of *Uno e 50*

CHAPTER I

The Family

IT WAS NOT long ago that country people in Valle di Comino in central Italy were illiterate. Before the Second World War, children had some education, at least to be able to read and write. Then war brought misery and hunger. There was no time for school where this story is set, in the town of Picinisco. This area of Italy had been very much affected by the Battle of Monte Cassino. With many civilian casualties, it had taken ten years for things to return to normal for the citizens of the valley. The country people did not know much of the world; some did not even know what was over the mountains. Their whole world was their house, their brothers and sisters and extended family. They knew all about the surrounding towns and villages, and all the family connections, because, to them, talking was a pleasure and a pastime. Aside from the local gossip, they got to know things that would help them to make a living.

This tale is about a large family: a mother and father, his parents and her mother, and their sixteen children. Andrea, the eldest, was twenty-four years old. Concettina, the eldest girl, was twenty. She had nine brothers and seven sisters. Bruno, the youngest, was two, and the mother pregnant.

How they lived was simple; they had the basics of life, the very basics. To put food on the table every day for twenty-one souls was not easy, but it was a joint effort. It meant everyone had something to do, from the youngest to the eldest. They scraped a living in their few acres of stony land, with their few animals. To keep these animals alive was a constant fight and the temptation to eat them was also a struggle.

In comparison with their neighbours, their house was big enough. It had four rooms downstairs, four rooms on the first floor and attic where they stored their grain. The house did not belong to the family, but to the mother's brother Alfonso, who had emigrated to America. After five years they heard nothing more from him, so his sister, with an ever-growing family, decided to move into the house with the approval of her mother.

The ground floor of the house had a very large kitchen, with a fireplace and a brick oven in one corner. In the middle of the room there were two huge tables placed end to end with chairs, stools and benches, but still there were not enough seats for the family. The very young children sat on the floor to eat their meal. The rest of the ground floor rooms were used to stable the animals and to store firewood, hay and foodstuffs.

Of the four rooms upstairs, only three were usable – the other room was open to the elements, with no window panes and a hole in the roof. It was fortunate that the rooms were all large because to accommodate such a large family, young and old, was not an easy task. But at least they were warm with the heat that came from their bodies; they slept close, man and wife.

Vincenzo Valente and his wife Matilda slept in one

room with the baby in their bed and the twin girls, Erica and Lia, were squeezed into the crib which they had outgrown long ago. Baths were an unheard-of luxury. The girls would take a large basin of hot water to their room and wash all over with a cloth and rough soap – and where they could not reach, there was always a sister to help. The life of the children at home was like a chain reaction: each was one of the links and those just a little older would help the younger ones. They were not really brought up, they were dragged up. How could it be otherwise? How could the parents cope with sixteen children and another on the way? God bless them all.

The family had a few acres of land in little patches here and there, some so far away it would take all morning to get there. But time was one thing the family had. Three or four of the siblings would set off and what needed to be done was done, after which they enjoyed a leisurely walk home. On their way, they would meet others – there was always time for fun, games and catching up with friends.

Everyone had a job to do. The grandfather and grandmothers kept the fire going, chopped wood, gathered tinder, fed the hens and the pigs: that was their domain.

Concettina and her sister Maria would help their mother to make bread every three days. The mother would oversee the task, making sure that everything was done to her liking. But it was the girls that would knead the heavy dough, one at one end of the deep wooden trough, one at the other end, four hands pulling and stretching, the warm dough up to their elbows.

Sometimes they would stop to straighten their backs, wipe the sweat from their flushed faces, then carry on until the dough was ready for its first rest. It was covered with a warm blanket until it was ready for its second kneading, then made into large two-kilo loafs, covered with the blanket again and left to rise. In the meantime, Nonno Andrea would light the huge brick oven and feed it with bundles of twigs, the prunings of the olive trees and a few chunks of heavy wood to keep the fire going until it was the right temperature to bake the bread.

The father would make sure that they cultivated their plots of land to the fullest. He would send a squad of the younger children to remove surface stones before ploughing. Then, after ploughing, the children would go again to remove all other stones that the plough had turned over. Some were so big that it took two strong boys to carry them to the edge of the field; these bigger stones were left there to reinforce the supporting terrace and stop their land from sliding down the hill. Then it was up to the children to dig with spades, right up to the edge of their property, so as not to waste a single inch of their land. Land was bread and bread was life.

The women at home were tasked to prepare two meals every day for the large family. It was never ending. The family would return to eat no matter where they happened to be.

CHAPTER 2

The Tarttaglia Family

BECAUSE THERE WERE so many mouths to feed, the Valente family also worked ground that belonged to the local landowner. Don Stefano came from a well-to-do family that had owned an estate in the area for centuries. It was said that his family originally came from Spain and that they were gifted the estate from the King of Naples. Whether this was true or just a legend nobody knew, but it made no difference – when the men passed him, they tipped their hats and the women curtseyed.

The Tarttaglia family lived in a *palazzo* (mansion) on the top of a hill. Lime trees lined the road that led to its iron gates. The gates were always open so that wagons and carts full of produce could pass through to its grain store. The silos were full to overflowing on good years and nearly empty on bad years. Some years, the farmers would have no money to buy the seed to sow the land, and the factor would give them some, for which they would pay when the new harvest came in. This would happen again and again until the loan was called in, and the only way to pay it was to sell a piece of their own land at a rock bottom price to the Tarttaglia family until there was nothing left, leaving farmers totally dependent on *il signore* on the hill. Then whatever they produced on the land that they had once owned would be halved. It was back-breaking work to produce enough for their large family and enough to fill the landlords' coffers to overflowing.

Some farmers had to abandon the land altogether and work as labourers for the estate. But it was always as day labourers; if there was work, they would be paid, if not, there would be no pay and they would have to look elsewhere, a day here, a day there. Sometimes they went further afield, as far as Rome or over the Abruzzi mountains to Pescasseroli, doing seasonal work: picking grapes, scything wheat, harvesting potatoes or gathering olives. The men would come back on Sundays to pass on their meagre wage to their wives. Then they would go back again on Monday.

The bodies of the men were scrawny, sun-baked and dark. Their teeth were black from smoking rough tobacco. But if they were in good health, there was always a twinkle in their eyes and if there was a laugh to be had they were ready for it. And when they went back home, they would enjoy their wives. The young men were virile and fertile and another child to feed would be conceived.

That year there was seed. Vincenzo was behind the plough and his two cows were attached to the harness, pulling with all their might and turning the earth over ready for the seed. His sons Andrea and Francesco followed behind, breaking up the clods of earth. Giovanni was leading the animals, pulling at the halter, and his sister Teresa and his younger brother Osvaldo were turning over the earth. It was hard work, back-breaking work; the sun was hot and tiring. Teresa kept looking at the sun – it was surely midday, time for her mother to bring food.

Eventually, Teresa saw three figures walking towards

them in the distance, her mother and younger sisters, Stefania and Fiorinda. The workers put down their tools and made their way to the edge of the field where there was some shade.

Matilda and her daughters arrived and set down the basket that they carried. Food for them, and hay and water for the animals. Andrea and Francesco saw to the beasts while their mother ladled the food onto plates. *Sagne e fagioli*, homemade pasta with beans, and a few stray bits of *cotechino*, rough pork sausage made with pig skin. This was, of course, followed by bread and cheese.

The family made themselves comfortable to eat. They were always hungry; although food was plentiful, the sheer number in the house made it impossible for them to feel truly satisfied. When they finished, Vincenzo took his tobacco and paper out of his pocket. Slowly and skilfully, licking the paper with the tip of his tongue, he made a perfect cigarette. Andrea, his eldest son, looked on greedily. If only he could have one too, but his father did not know that he smoked whenever he could get one. If he asked his father for a cigarette, he would get a blow on the back of his head. Vincenzo, although he was a smoker himself, did not want the boys to get into the habit. He was always telling them that it was bad for their health and for their pocket.

Vincenzo inhaled deeply, blowing the smoke out of his nose.

He finished his cigarette, threw the stub away and got up to resume ploughing the land. The boys followed him, disappointed, because usually they could lie down in the shade and rest a little after their meal before they went back to their toil.

Matilda called him back. 'Vincenzo, on my way here I met Don Pasquale. He said that he had spoken to Donna Tarttaglia – she asked him if he knew of a good clean girl to work at the house as a maid and he has suggested Teresa. I said to him that I was sure that Teresa would be very happy to go, what do you think?'

Teresa was looking from her mother to her father.

'Yes, yes! I want to go!' she exclaimed. Anything to get out of the house.

Her mother ignored her and spoke again to her husband, 'What do you think?'

Vincenzo's first thought was yes, one less at home, but, on reflection, he did not know if it was a good idea. He looked at Teresa – she was the prettiest of his girls. Fresh face, a golden glow to her skin, plenty of dark hair and a good figure. Would she be safe away from home?

'Do you want to go? Remember, if you do, you will be at their beck and call all day. It won't be like when you are at home where you please yourself and avoid chores if you can. All I hear when I am home is your mother calling you – you are never there when you are wanted.'

'Yes, Papà, I want to go. I am sure I will learn many things in the big house, and I will work really hard, make myself indispensable to Donna Tarttaglia, you will see. I will make you proud of me.'

'All right, then go, you know your way home.'

His wife then said, addressing Teresa, 'The priest said that he will come tomorrow morning, he will take you to the house. *La signora* wants to see you first.'

Seeing her daughter's excitement, Matilda raised her eyebrows and added with a wry smile, 'Don't get your hopes up too high, she may not like you when she sees your *capo alerto*, arrogance.'

Teresa implored first her father then her mother with a look. 'Please can I go home now to get ready?'

Her father looked at the flushed, excited girl with her good looks and charming way. She always got what she wanted.

'If you must, then go.'

Matilda and Teresa packed away the remainder of their meal and went home, where Teresa spent the rest of the day getting ready. She washed her hair and prepared the clothes she wanted to wear the following day, hoping to make a good impression on Donna Beatrice. The rest of the family slowly made their way back to their work.

Andrea was in a foul mood. He picked up the rake and pulled and pushed at the clods of earth, smoothing the soil into a fine tilth ready for the wheat seed.

All the while, he talked to himself and to his brother Francesco, who was beside him. 'Why is it that we have to work like beasts of burden, like mules. Look at us breaking our backs to do this work by hand. Tomorrow we will go to Cesidio's farm to do it all over again. He is a wealthy man, he owns a large farm, why does he not buy a tractor? He has the money. But no, he uses us as cheap labour. I tell you, brother, if I had the money, I would buy a tractor. I would use it on our land and other people's land and charge a fee per hour. At least I would be sitting, driving the tractor, not breaking my back like this.'

In his frustration he kicked the earth. He hated the earth.

'You are right,' said Francesco, 'times are changing. We can't go on like this, we have to do something.'

Andrea continued, 'I am going to leave home, I will either go up north and work in the factories or emigrate, I don't care where to. Zio Alfonso is in America, but we have not heard from him in years. Maybe I could go to England, or France or even Germany, where you can choose where you want to work. They are rebuilding the cities that were bombed during the war. One thing is for sure, I am not going to spend the rest of my life making a living from the dirt,' and he again kicked a lump of earth. The good earth did not deserve it, it had eased the hunger of many before him.

He stopped for breath, looking around him, looking for inspiration. He could see his sisters Stefania and Fiorinda, as brown as berries and singing in harmony while they worked, used to the hot sun. But he knew from experience that their joyful, happy youth would not last long. Within five years of getting married, they would already have three children and any trace of their former youth would have vanished.

CHAPTER 3

Andrea. Francesco. Pietro.

AFTER A SEVERE WINTER, spring was in the air. The trees were adorned with delicate, pale green leaves. Some were already in flower, the pear, apple, plum and, of course, the cherry trees. Everyone hoped that there would be no more freezing cold spells to ruin the blossoms on the trees. Fruit was their dessert, fruit was what they craved; its sweet flesh was such a treat to them.

Now that the nights were not so cold, there were not so many people trying to get close to the fire. The grandparents had priority, often with a child or two on their lap.

Dinner was cooking. Matilda, Concettina and Maria were seeing to it. *Le nonne* were both busy preparing a huge basket of the first of the new season *broccoletti*, garlic and *peperoncino* (chilli pepper), all chopped and ready to drop in a pot of green olive oil. The smell was delicious. Soon, the meal was over and the *broccoletti* had been enjoyed by everyone. They used bread to mop up all the garlicky oil.

It was their routine that, after dinner, the parents would give out instructions and tasks for the following day. They were going to work for Cesidio and Vincenzo wanted to establish who was able to go, and who had other tasks to do.

Andrea could not stand to hear it, all this work and for what? He did not stay to listen to his father. He pushed his chair back and got up, saying that he was going out, and jumped on an old, battered bike that was lying outside. He pedalled hard to climb up the hill, but once he was on the high road to Colle Posta he flew downhill all the way to the bar in Villa Latina. He could see that some of his friends were already there.

The bar was full, although it did not take many people to fill it up because the inside space was small. Three or four tables were already taken up by elderly customers who would sit to play a game of cards. Others would stand at the counter with a drink in hand, while those who would have liked a drink but did not have the money would stand about hoping that someone would offer.

As soon as Andrea walked in, his friend Fernando called to him.

'Want a drink, what will it be?'

'No, I have just finished eating. I had a few glasses of wine, *Sto bene*, I'm okay thanks.'

Andrea said this in a casual way, trying not to show that he had a troubled mind. He would have liked a beer, but he knew that he could not return the favour. He was a proud man. He stood about for a while talking to the men and the boys in the bar. He knew them all and they knew him. They knew of his circumstances as he knew of theirs. That was the problem of living in small *paese* like Picinisco and Villa Latina – you would be judged in what you did, and what you did not do. That was the nature of the beast.

In a couple of weeks, it would be warm enough to sit on the terrace outside of the bar. They would start to sell ice cream, which would attract the women and children to come and sit outside with friends. Andrea would feel more comfortable coming to the bar as people came and went without feeling obliged to buy anything. He noticed that his friend Fernando and some other youths were all standing around a man. They seemed to be listening to him intently, which was unusual; normally in the bar everyone would jostle everyone else to be the one doing all the talking – often a lot of nonsense. Andrea made his way over to listen.

***

Back in the house, after Andrea had stormed off in a temper, the others in the family also went their own way.

Francesco and Pietro both had girlfriends – they each had a quick wash, changed into clean clothes and left. Pietro did not have far to go, he only had to walk up the track. Five minutes and he was there. His heart was already racing just at the thought that he would soon be with her.

Anna was the daughter of a shepherd. The family came from Fontitune, a small village on the side of the mountain. It was a village so high up that in winter it was above the snow line, and so the people had to relocate to somewhere else in the valley where they would rent a house for the family and stables for the animals. The house that Anna's father had rented was just a shack with two rooms, but it had the basics: a fireplace, a brick oven, wooden shutters on the window and a door with gaps at the side. It had no running water, but it did have electric lights.

When they had first arrived, Franco, Anna's father, had come to ask if they could take water from their well. That was the beginning of a friendship between the two families. They were always ready to help each other. It was also the start of a give and take, which was the common courtesy between country folk. Neighbours would share: if one family had a surplus of vegetables, at that time it was *broccoletti*, you would send it to your family and neighbours, and they would do the same for you when they had more than they could use. This was even more common with Franco and Vincenzo's households because Franco had cheese, ricotta, sometimes meat and whey, a by-product of cheese making, which Pietro would collect to feed to the pigs. In exchange, Matilda would send vegetables that were in season. Sometimes she would send *panettone* or biscuits if she had baked. Vincenzo would go to Franco with a bottle of wine and they would sit outside to share a drink and exchange life stories. Franco had three daughters. Anna, the eldest, was eighteen years old. She and her sisters, Silvia and Patrizia, became good friends with the members of the Valente family.

When Pietro arrived at the house, he could see his girl in the stables helping her father, who was milking the sheep and goats. He was doing this by sitting on a three-legged stool beside a small opening to the stable. As a sheep was whipped towards the opening, he would grab it by its hind leg and then by its udder to milk it. The milk would spurt into the pail between his legs.

Anna was there with a whipping branch, making the sheep stand to wait their turn.

It was just getting dark and as he approached her, he could see that she was continuously looking down the track. It made his heart leap that she was looking for him.

He jumped over the fence, 'I am here, *amore*!' he said. They stood for a moment looking at each other, a look of longing just to embrace.

Anna laughed as she chased a sheep round the pen. Pietro watched her. She was beautiful: lips that drove him to madness, eyes that sparkled in the dim twilight, a full womanly body.

'Pietro, is that you?'

Pietro jumped. He felt that Anna's father had read his mind.

'Yes, Zio Franco, it is me.'

'Could you give me the other pail and take this one away, it's already full.'

When the milking was finished, they each carried a pail of milk and went indoors. The family had not yet had their meal; they usually ate much later than Pietro's family. Pietro would try not to come until he knew that they had eaten, but it was hard to wait that extra hour before he could come up. It was as if an irresistible force was pulling him to her – he just had to be with her.

He had met Anna in the autumn when her family had arrived to live in Colle Poste for the winter. She would come every day to fetch water from the well, sometimes with her sisters. All three girls enjoyed coming for water because, in his house, there was always someone to talk to. Chatting was the favourite pastime for the people of the countryside. Pietro would flirt with all three girls. He was always on the lookout to see if one of the girls was at the well.

Then he noticed that he tended to look for Anna and would be disappointed when it was not her getting water. When it was Anna, he would drop everything and go to watch her. She would throw the bucket to the bottom of the well where it would fill up with water. Then she pulled it up. This was done manually, hand over hand, making a pile of chain in front of her, and once the bucket came up, she would pour the water into the plastic container. Pietro was fascinated watching her do this. It had a certain rhythm, feet planted firmly on the ground, and every time she lifted her arm high up to pull on the chain, he could see the full roundness of her breast. He would go over and offer to carry the container to the house for her.

Her body became an irresistible fantasy for him; her long slender neck had a beauty spot on the pulse and he could see its slight movement as she talked to him; her full bosom; her hips that flared out from her slim waist. He could not see her legs because she wore her skirt long. Sometimes if he was walking behind her up the steep track, she would bend down to pick a wild gladiolus that grew at that time of the year at the side of the road, and he would catch just a glimpse of the back of her knees which would send his pulse racing.

After a while, he noticed that it was always Anna that came for the water, which gave him hope that perhaps she felt for him what he felt for her. Eventually, he plucked up the courage to ask her to *fare l'amore* with him, which was the old-fashioned way to ask a girl if he could court her. She shyly said that she would ask her mother. From then on, he went to her house every night to be with her.

Courting Anna was frustrating. Her parents were old-fashioned, as were all the mountain folk. They watched their daughter, always aware of where she was. If occasionally they were permitted to go to the cinema since it had reopened after being destroyed in the war, all three sisters had to go. Anna, now that she was courting, was always accompanied wherever she went.

For the girls of the valley, things were changing. The clothes they wore were more modern: wide, short skirts which flared out when they danced, the new dance of the moment which they loved. They never could get enough of rock and roll. They would go to the cinema in groups, boys and girls, and to feel very modern some of the girls had cut their hair short in the latest style.

A new paper mill had just opened in Ponte Melfa and was taking on girls. Those that were allowed were delighted to go – you would see them in the mornings setting off on their bikes as happy as if they going to *alla festa* (a festival). They were happy; happy to get a wage at the end of the month which they would hand to their parents; happy to be able to buy new clothes, pretty blouses and skirts which they would wear with at least two or three underskirts to make it flare out. In the post-war years, there was at last an air of optimism, at least for the girls.

When the meal was ready, Franco, his wife Benedetta and the three girls would sit to eat. Both mother and father would urge Pietro to eat with them, they would go on and on for him to take something. He would take a piece of cheese just to please them and the meal would end. Pietro and Anna would sit with the rest of the family, talking of this and that. There was always something to say. Pietro would be asked about his family, about the things that needed to be done on the land. They would gossip about people that they knew.

Eventually the conversation would dry up, with Pietro giving the shortest answers possible to the questions. The courting couple could not wait for the moment when her father would stand up and say, 'I am off to bed now, good night.'

Silvia and Patrizia followed their father, giving Anna a coy smile. The mother would also go, but the courting couple knew that she would not go to sleep. She would sit on a chair in her bedroom, knitting.

Alone at last, they sat close at the table holding hands, heads touching, whispering to each other what lovers have always whispered.

Benedetta, after a while, would call that it was time for bed. 'Anna, don't be too long!'

Anna would then accompany Pietro outside on his way home. They shared a kiss, but this time with fierce passion, embracing their bodies close.

Then Anna would push him away, say, 'Goodnight, my love,' and run into the house before her mother called her again.

Pietro would wait outside in the dark looking at the

house, waiting for Anna to come to the window for one last wave and to blow kisses. He would not leave until she eventually put out the light and, even then, he would wait for one last wave and flying kiss.

As Pietro walked home that night, he was resolute. Tomorrow, he was going to speak with Anna's father, ask him if he could marry his daughter. He knew that soon they would move back up the mountain to their village. Fontitune was far away – he could not go every night as he did now and the thought that he would not see her every day was unbearable. He sat by the well to think about what to do. He would speak to his father, tell him that he wanted to get married. Then he thought, Anna's family were moving out of the house soon, maybe he could rent it. He knew that the rental was cheap and at least they would have a roof over their heads. To bring his wife to his house was unthinkable – there was just no room. Yes, he thought, that is what he would do.

Tomorrow he would propose to his love. He would go to the barber to have his hair cut, he would ask Concettina to iron his shirt. It would be nice to bring her roses. She loved flowers, she was always picking wildflowers to bring home to put in a vase. Then his thoughts turned to more practical matters. What did he have to offer her? Nothing apart from his undying love, but how could they live on that? He wanted to marry as soon as possible, but he could not do that – not at least until he had a job where he would get a wage every month. He knew that a new soap factory was about to open in Picinisco and was looking for workers. He would go first thing in the morning. He started thinking of anyone he knew who could put in a good word for him.

Pietro was sitting beside the well, but with so many things on his mind he felt unable to go indoors to sleep. He decided to go to the bar, where he would meet some of his friends as well as his brother Andrea. On his way home, he could speak to his brother about his plans.

***

Francesco had a bit further to go to see his girl. He had to walk up the hill. His family's house was in a hollow between two ridges; on the top of one ridge was the little village of San Pietro and on the other was a little hamlet called Colle Posta. The high road that went to the town of Picinisco passed through Colle Posta. Once Francesco had walked up the track to Colle Posta, he had the choice to either turn right and make the long climb to Picinisco or turn left and walk down to Villa Latina.

Villa Latina, at that time, had everything that you would want of a small town: it had two bars, an emporium that sold everything and was the hub of the place, and also a hostel with a few rooms where you could stop to have a rough meal or stay the night. The owners of the emporium, Rosina and her husband Alberto, had six daughters that helped with the work, serving at the counters and also waiting at tables in the tavern. They were all lively, fun-loving girls that kept the place buzzing. The eldest girl was twenty-two and the youngest was fourteen, so they were at the ages to be troublesome to their parents, especially their mother; their father had long ago given up any hope that he could control the nine women that were in his house, including the two maids. For him, the only good thing about having six daughters was that it was good for business.

He had longed for a son. Every time his wife was expecting, he would get his hopes up – this time, surely, it would be a boy. Then, disappointment... another girl. Even now, after all this time, he would say to his wife, 'We are still young, let us try again.' Maybe seven was his lucky number. But his wife was completely against it. Not after fourteen years – to start all over again with a baby would be too much.

'Just wait for a grandson now,' she would laugh. She was happy with her six daughters and would not change even one of them for anything, including a boy. Her house was always full of friends, and boyfriends were always calling. Any excuse for a dance. Now that they had the radio and the gramophone, there was music in the house. The girls knew the words of the songs and would sing along. They were great girls. Her girls.

The only thing that troubled her was that the three eldest were *fidanzate* (had boyfriends), so it was hard to keep track of them, to see what they were up to when they went out. It was much easier in the past when courting was done at home. She was worried that one day one of the girls would come to tell her what no mother wanted to hear. She knew that her husband would blame her because he was always saying that she was far too lenient with the girls, but times were changing, and for the better, she thought.

Rosina was just about to close the shop when Francesco walked in.

'*Ciao*,' he said, and seeing that she was going upstairs, added, 'is there anything I can do for you?'

She was carrying a tray with cakes as well as the cash box.

'I'll carry that for you,' he said as he took the box from her.

Rosina looked at the handsome, flushed youth and smiled at him. He really was exceptionally handsome – she could see why her daughter had lost her head over him. But really, what else had he to offer her? She did not know how his folks were able to put food on the table for all of them. As he walked into the kitchen, a modern kitchen with cupboards and a large gas cooker with an oven underneath, he could see the family were all there and the table was laid.

'Stay and eat with us Francesco,' said Alberto. Alberto always greeted his daughter's boyfriend in a friendly way. He was glad to have male company.

'*Grazie*, I have already eaten, but I was wondering if Catarina wanted to go for a *passeggiata*, a nice walk. The evening is warm and mellow, and the days are so much longer that now we will be back before dark.'

He looked at Catarina hoping that she would help him to convince her father. Instead, his wife replied, 'Yes, but she must eat first.'

Catarina ran to get a cardigan and was halfway out

of the door, telling her parents that she was not at all hungry. Francesco wished everyone goodnight and followed Catarina out.

Villa Latina was different from all the other towns in the valley because it was not situated on high ground, on a hill or at the side of the mountains surrounding the valley. It was on the valley floor. The high road ran right through it, and the main part of the village, the houses, bars, shops and a paved walkway where the people went for a *passeggiata*, to see and to be seen, sat along the roadside. Villa Latina did have a *piazza* and a church in the old part of the town, but people preferred the bright lights of the main road. There was more life. People came to shop, too: there was a butcher, barber, hairdresser and of course the emporium which sold everything.

The couple were walking along the road where they would meet like-minded friends, also on a refreshing evening walk. They were happy. They looked at each other in delight, walking side by side, close but not quite touching. They would have liked to hold hands, but it was not allowed, at least not in public. The young couple did make a beautiful pair. Francesco was tall, his body in perfect proportion, nice thick black hair, dark eyes and a lovely smile. Catarina had fallen for that smile, hook, line and sinker – she was in love and it showed. She was radiant as she walked at his side. Her whole body moved as she talked – she would look at him with big eyes, unable to keep her arms down at her sides. Gesticulating as she spoke, her body would swing from side to side making her skirt dance. Occasionally, she would let out a squeal of laughter; she found everything funny. If they met another couple, they would stop for a while, then move on. They wanted to be alone. They went as far as they could, then walked back slowly, waiting for darkness when Francesco would take her hand and pull her into a dark niche to kiss her. She would return the kiss with equal passion. They were in love. A *far l'amore* the old-fashioned way, when kisses burned because that was as far as it went.

Once Francesco had accompanied Catarina to her door and bid her a heated goodnight, he went to the bar to see if any of his brothers were there. He could see his brother Andrea deep in conversation with a well-groomed and stylishly dressed man. Pietro was also there with a beer in his hand, talking to the mayor of Picinisco. Francesco joined Andrea and he sat down to listen in on the conversation.

Andrea looked at his brother and said, 'Tony, this is my brother Francesco,' then he and Tony went on with what they were talking about.

'As I was saying,' continued Tony, 'when I first emigrated to Scotland, it was with the intention to go for a few years, make some money and come back, but the longer I stayed the more I liked it. I began to learn the language, I got used to the climate, the people were kind. My *patrone* was good to me, I would get my wage at the end of the month and the work was easy and involved things that I already knew working on the farm with animals. Soon, I was driving the tractor. My boss liked that; he could see that I was a hard worker.'

'You would not believe how good the food was. I ate with them, whatever they had I had and as much as I wanted. The wife would ask if I wanted more – I was too shy to say "yes" because she had already given me a large portion, but it was that good,' he laughed. 'They have this thing they call porridge, with fresh cream taken straight off the top of the milk with honey to sweeten it, then toast dripping with butter. That would be for breakfast. At night there would be meat, roast beef, *carne cosi buone*, so good, and after the meat course they always have a sweet pudding, like apple pie with custard and cream. They eat that pudding hot, it is so good, and just to finish about food, at lunchtime there would be a pile of sandwiches, fruit, cheese and beer they made themselves.'

Tony could see that the boys were impressed, listening with mouths open, and he went on to talk about more serious things.

'I worked on the farm for my full contract of four years. My boss was so disappointed when I told him that I was leaving when my contract ended. I was upset too, I felt I was letting him down after they had been so good to me. But I could not stay. Other *paesani* (Italians) who were in the city were all doing well in jobs that paid good money, others had saved money and were able to put down a deposit to buy a fish and chip shop, or a café, or *gelateria*.

'Other young men like me had met and married girls from this area who had gone to work there as a *domestiche*. I wanted to do the same – why not, if they could do it... why could I not do it too? And that's what I did. I lodged with a family called Crolla, I got a job working in a fish and chip shop, *pesce e patate*, and I learned the trade. But I had to start at the bottom. I started peeling and chopping many sacks of potatoes, every morning ten sacks. Of course, they have machines to do that. I also had to cut and bone large quantities of fish, then take bins of chipped potatoes upstairs where the cooking was done. When all had been done down in the cellar, at night I would help to fry. I quickly learned and from then on I just worked upstairs. I worked for these people for two years. Then I heard that this person, again a Crolla, had a shop to rent. I quickly went to see him, my pocket full of the money I had saved so I could make him an offer there and then, cash in hand. I was so happy I had my own shop. I did everything properly to improve it. I had learned a lot from my employer, the shop was always spotless and I always had on a clean white apron. Then, I thought, I have my own shop now I can marry and have a family of my own. I tell you boys, it was a great feeling when I got the keys to my shop. I felt I was on top of the world, thinking about what I left behind and what I have now. I can look a girl in the face and ask her to marry me. I have come back to my *paese* to find a girl. There are plenty Italian girls in Edinburgh, but I want a wife from my own town. That way you know what you are getting, you know what I mean!' he laughed and called for another beer.

'Anyway,' he went on, 'I have fallen for a pretty wee thing and she is the girl for me, a bit young but she will learn quickly. I am getting married next week, then I will leave her. I need to go back because I left the shop in someone else's hands, but once all the papers are ready my wife will come to Scotland too. There is no stopping me now – I am looking for another shop, maybe two,' he slapped the table with a roar of laughter.

This was the opportunity that Andrea was looking for. He said, 'You will need someone to work for you if you get two shops. How about me? I want to get away from this misery of a town and from this country – I mean it, I am not joking.'

Tony looked at Andrea. He could see the glint of excitement in his eye. Why not, he thought. One person can only do so much; if he was going to be running two shops, he would need help. He remembered the old saying, 'you will never get rich only working with your own arms'.

'If you are serious, we can talk about it,' he said. 'But you know that *La Gran Bretagna* will not let you into the country unless you have five pounds. Do you have five pounds?'

'Sure I have five pounds, no problem!'

'*Va bene*, okay, I have to go now but we will talk later.'

He got up to go, paid for the drinks, taking a wad of cash out of his pockets. Andrea thanked him for the drinks and said to him, 'Will I see you here tomorrow night?'

Tony answered, 'I don't know about tomorrow because, as I said, I am getting married. But don't worry, I will be in touch with you, okay.' And with a '*Buona Sera a tutti*', he left.

The three brothers were soon on their way home. Francesco said to Andrea, 'Are you really serious, you want to emigrate?'

'Yes, why not? What is there for me here? You heard him, there are many more opportunities abroad. If you work hard, you will get places, what do you get here apart from a broken back? Yes, I have made up my mind, I am going either with Tony or someone else. I will walk there if I must. The problem is, where will I get five pounds? I think that is about fifteen thousand lira. Mamma and Papà can't help me – I know that they are going to sell the calves, but that money has to last all year. It's the only cash they have, I can't take it, that is out of the question. Pietro, you said that you want to get married. They will need money for your wedding. I have to think of something else, rob a bank maybe.'

The brothers laughed as they walked on, each talking of their problems and making light of it as young, robust, healthy young men will do.

CHAPTER 4

Andrea Has a Problem

THE NEXT DAY Andrea could not get the conversation he had with Tony at the bar out of his mind. He went over and over it. Is that what he should do, start a new life like him? He did want to go, but he was scared. He did not have any knowledge of the language and he had heard people at the bar talking at full speed in another tongue. He did not know if they were speaking in English, French or German. Would he be able to learn a new language? He was twenty-four – was he too old to pick it up? When he was at school, he was not the brightest boy in the class. He went to the stable to harness the horse, took an axe and saw, mounted the beast and set off.

It was a beautiful spring day, a perfect day for woodcutting. As the horse trotted along, he passed San Pietro on the ridge, then down and up again. He soon reached the *piazza* at Le Serre with its little chapel in ruins. If you turned down the road, it would take you to Valle Grande; if you went up the road it would take you to I Ciacca. He went towards I Ciacca, there you would start the climb to Collerute and from there, after a few miles, you would arrive in Picinisco.

The family had a couple of acres of woodland just past I Ciacca. To get there was difficult – there was a narrow path along the base of the hill then a steep climb where he had to dismount the horse to walk on foot.

At one point along the path there was a turning that went to a ramshackle house, a couple of rooms side by side, each with an outside door. He could see some chickens searching and clucking around the place and two goats in a pen. The owner of the place, Isabella, came out, throwing a bucket of water outside. He was hoping that she had not seen him, but she had and was walking towards him.

She was a woman in her thirties, who at one time in her youth must have been beautiful. She was still a beauty, like a rose in full bloom, but about to lose its petals.

The woman came towards him, all dishevelled, her hair partly held up with a clasp. Her blouse had missing buttons and her skirt was too short for her. On her feet she wore flip flops.

'*Whey! Beglio guaglione*, hello handsome, *da quando tempo*... long time no see. I have just made a pot of coffee, come have a cup, sit down for a bit, you know what they say, coffee should be drunk hot, in company and sitting down.'

'Where is your husband, is he not here to share a cup of coffee with you?'

'No, Antonio was hired for a few days' work in Ferentino. It is too far for him to come home every day, so he is staying there. The *patrone* has a caravan that they sleep in, he won't be back until Friday.'

Andrea tied the horse to a post and went towards Isabella, '*Va bene*, a coffee sounds good.'

Once in the kitchen, Isabella took the coffee pot off the shelf, filling it first with water then the coffee, then a tight squeeze to close *la Napoletana*.

'You said the coffee was ready.'

'This way it will be hot, you know it can be very lonely up here, not many people pass by. It's nice to see a face, especially one as good looking as yours, *belli come te*.' She laughed and sat down pulling her skirt up as she did.

The coffee was ready, two cups, two teaspoons of sugar in each and a good stir. She brought the coffee to the table, leaning over as she put it in front of him.

Andrea had hardly said ten words to her, but all his senses were alert to her every movement. It seemed to him that everything she did was exciting – when she filled the cup, when she stirred the sugar, when she sat down, when she walked, when she leaned over the table to put the cup in front of him, her breast hanging down ready to be cupped in your hand.

'Drink your coffee, it's there in front of you.'

She sat opposite him, coffee cup in her hands. She looked at him with a bemused smile on her face.

He managed to say in an odd voice that he did not recognise as his own, 'So Antonio is coming back on Friday?'

'Yes,' she said looking him straight in the eye.

'I'd better go now, thanks for the coffee.'

'Stay a bit longer.'

'No, no, I must go, it's getting late. See you later.'

Andrea left and he was halfway to the woods when he remembered the horse. He had to go back for it, he could hear her laughing.

The young man scrambled up the steep track that

led to his part of the woodland. The horse followed him on the rein. Once there, he tied it to a tree with a long rope so that it could crop the herbage. Then he set to work to look through the woods. If he saw any branch that was damaged or dead, he would climb the tree and cut it down. The branches that he could not reach, he had to pull down with a rope. The rope had a weight at the end, and he would throw the weight over the dead branch and pull so it would come crashing down. The woodland was only a couple of acres, but if well managed as Nonno Andrea had shown them, there was enough firewood for their needs. The trees were kept healthy by doing what he was doing now. In late autumn, when the trees had lost their leaves, they would cut away all surplus growth, cut a mature tree or two, see which sapling to encourage and which to cut down. All the cut wood would lie on the ground until the end of winter, when it would be sorted and sawed into manageable pieces. Nothing was wasted, including the branches, and his father would hire a muleteer, a man who had a string of mules, to bring the firewood home.

Andrea worked hard, sweat pouring off him. He was taking his frustrations out on the work at hand. At last, from sheer tiredness, he calmed down, prepared a load of fuel to take home and loaded up the horse ready to go. He was thinking to himself, if only there was another way to go home. He knew that Isabella would be waiting for him. She would be at the well, either doing the washing, leaning over the trough with her bum in the air where he could see to the top of her leg or hanging the clothes out to dry; or with one foot in the trough to wash her feet; or her blouse off washing her hair. He knew that she did it on purpose to torture him. His eyes were drawn to her, though he couldn't help but look to see if her husband was around.

But her husband was away. Should he try his luck? Or was she the type that would tempt you to madness, then as soon as you did something she would cry rape or even worse tell her husband that you made a pass at her. He could put money on it, that she would have her blouse off and be washing her hair just because her husband was away.

No, he would have lost the money. She had her skirt pulled up to her thighs, one foot in the trough washing her leg.

'Andrea, do you want a drink of water? It's nice and cold from the well.'

'*Sto bene*, no I'm fine, see you later.'

He walked away, the horse clip-clopping behind him.

'Antonio will not be back till Friday!'

The look in her eye when she said that!

Today was Tuesday – oh, fuck her! – he thought as he tried to get rid of the picture of her with her skirt pulled up to wash her leg.

No, he would go to the bar, see if Tony was there. He had to get away from there or he was going to kill someone. Then his thoughts went back to Isabella. What was the worst that could happen if he went back tomorrow to get another load of firewood?

Husband coming back to find them 'at it'. Husband

chasing him along the path with his shotgun. Isabella telling Antonio about what had happened, asking for forgiveness in tears. Antonio coming to find him in the woods to kill him. Worse still, Antonio at the bar, drunk as he often was, accusing him of raping his wife, wanting to beat him up. Andrea knew that he could flatten him with one blow. But then what had happened would be the talk of the town and his father would hear of it. Was he too old to be beaten up by his father? He would certainly get a thrashing if he was twenty or under.

The next day was Wednesday and Andrea's mind was elsewhere all day long. He checked the wood pile to see whether it was on the low side and it could do with more, if it needed stocked up.

'Papà, do you think it's going to rain today? Should I go for a load of wood before the lumber gets wet?'

It was Thursday. It was now or never. Fuck it, he was going. He was hoping to pass her house and not see her. Or did he want to see her?

There she was, sitting outside her house, trimming *broccoletti*.

She jumped when she saw him. 'Andrea, *bello mio*. Come and sit for a while, I am feeling very lonesome. Antonio is not coming home until tomorrow and not a soul passes by.'

Andrea felt sorry for the woman. He hitched the horse and went over and sat at the table. She said, 'Do you like *broccoletti*? I can give you some.'

'Thanks, but we have plenty at home. Are you missing Antonio?'

'No, not really. I just hope that he brings his pay

packet home. That he will not smoke or drink it all before he gets here.'

Under the table the young man's leg was getting a good rub from her foot. That's it, he thought. He put his hand on her thigh and let it lie there for a moment. He started to pull up her skirt. She didn't protest, he went a little higher, she opened her legs.

He could hardly get the words out, '…Do you want to?'

'Yes.'

'Let us go inside then.'

They did.

It was a couple of hours before he walked away. She was just as keen as he was. Just as he was about to go, he turned to give her a parting kiss. She looked happy and contented as she said to him, 'Thank you, Andrea,' which he thought was a strange thing to say.

The next day, Antonio came back. Then it was a game of cat and mouse. Was he at home? Was he working? Would he be away all day?

For two weeks they took their chances when they could. They could not resist. Their lovemaking was hot, passionate and quick.

One day Isabella said to Andrea, 'Tomorrow he is going to be away all day. He is going to visit his mother – usually when he goes there, he stays all day.' She reached up to give him a last caress, 'Come tomorrow, we can take it slow.'

The next day, he hitched the horse in the woods and walked back to Isabella who was waiting for him. After, they lay on the bed, enjoying the moment.

He was dressed, about to go out when, as he opened the door, he got the fright of his life and quickly shut it.

Antonio was outside, he was coming home. What was he going to do? The room had no window, just the front door going directly outside.

'What do I do, hide under the bed?'

Andrea was in such a panic, he wanted to run, but where?

Isabella said, 'I will go outside to distract him, you look for an opportunity to make a run for it behind the house.'

He did just that, a mad dash across a field, making a long detour before he could go back to where his horse was hitched. He loaded up the horse to go home. He would not push his luck. He would leave for Scotland as soon as possible.

* * *

The night before he was to leave for Scotland he was at the bar, his last night with his friends, when Antonio walked in.

Andrea's thoughts went straight to Isabella. Antonio is here. He had his bike outside. I Ciacca was quite far away. It would take him half an hour to get there, most of the way being uphill. Should he go to bid Isabella goodbye? What folly! His pulse was racing.

Antonio seemed to be in a really good state of mind, offering all his friends a drink. Andrea moved closer to listen to what he was saying before he set off.

'Yes,' Antonio was saying, 'after eight years of trying,

at last we have made it. She just told me this morning. My wife Isabella is expecting a baby. She is pregnant. Praise God.'

All at once Andrea sat down, all notion to visit Isabella gone... eight years trying and all at once she was pregnant.

CHAPTER 5

Teresa Goes to the *Palazzo*

TERESA WAS UP early so that she would have plenty of time to get ready before Don Pasquale arrived to take her to see *la signora* Beatrice. She combed her hair carefully, put on her ironed blouse and borrowed Maria's best shoes. Then she ate breakfast, a bowl of milky tea and a handful of biscotti. Her nonna really made the best biscotti. She would ask her if she could take a basketful to Donna Beatrice.

'Do you think that would be a nice thing to do, Mamma?' she asked her mother, who was in the kitchen with her, giving her a lecture on how she should behave. Always curtsey to Donna Beatrice, eyes down when she passed her sons, polite to Don Stefano, always put on an apron so her clothes would not get dirty. Neither the girl nor her mother knew what her duties would be – would it be housework or was she to work outside the house as well?

'Do you think I should ask her how much my pay will be or is that too presumptuous of me? Mamma, what do you think?'

Her mother thought for a minute then she said, 'Maybe you should when she has said that you are suitable and rings the bell for a servant to take you down to the kitchen. When you are about to walk away, turn back and say, "*Signora,* how much will my wage be, for my family is very much in need of it."

Maybe she will be generous and not take advantage of your youth, but whatever she says, say "*grazie*" and curtsy. Now don't exaggerate the curtsy, just a little bend of the knee and a little nod of the head, after all she is not the pope, and when you give her the biscotti say that Nonna Maria sent them with her compliments.'

Don Pasquale appeared at the door. 'Are you ready now, girlie? *Buongiorno* Matilda,' he said as he sat down. He was all out of breath.

'Have you got a drink for me Matilda? Just water will do at this time of the morning, I really do not know why I said I would come here for you, we could have met there. I had to walk all this way and I am not as fit as I used to be. Is that Maria's biscotti?' he said as he took one. 'She does make the best biscotti, if you will put some in a poke for me, Matilda, I will take them home to have later. I noticed as I walked here that you have spring greens already. Oh, there is nothing nicer than the first of the season of spring *broccoletti*.'

Before he had time to ask for some, Maria said, 'I will send one of the boys with a bag to your house. There is no point taking it with you now, you will have to carry it about all day. I will also send some eggs as well as the *broccoletti*.'

Don Pasquale was happy with that and turned to Teresa, 'Shall we go now? My, my, you are looking lovely, yes, yes you are beautiful just like your mother.' He stood up to go shaking the biscotti crumbs off his tunic and both priest and girl left.

The walk to the estate would take about half an

hour, but Teresa had to slow her pace to stay in step with the priest, so she walked slowly looking about her. Spring was here at last in all its glory, every shade of green spotted by a multitude of wildflowers, tulips, violets, the occasional daffodil and many others. She looked up to the mountains. They still had snow at the peaks. She loved this time of year.

She said to the priest, 'I love this time of the year, don't you? It just seems as if there is everything to look forward to.' Then she thought of the new job, she stopped for a minute and took a sniff of the violets she had in her hand.

'Father,' she said, 'do you think Donna Beatrice will like me? I do hope I will be in the house, I really don't want to go there to look after chickens. You will put in a good word for me, won't you? Please do.'

Don Pasquale looked at the girl tenderly, 'We will just have to wait and see, but remember that God is watching, so keep yourself to yourself and let no one interfere with you. Keep your mind free of sin and remember to come to confession every month. I will say that you are a good girl and I am sure you will be alright.'

By this time, they were walking up the road, lined with lime trees, that led to the house. The ditches by the roadside were full of spring greens for anyone with an eye to see, lamb's lettuce, dandelions and other edible herbs that her grandmother picked to include in her minestrone. There were flowers, gladiolus, wild orchids and yellow primroses. Teresa loved to see the coming to life of the countryside after the bleak winter. It seemed to her that the new sap in the earth was also coming to her through the soles of her feet. She wanted to run to her new adventure, to live in a *palazzo* even though it was only as a servant.

As they passed through the open gates, the road split into three. Straight ahead, with a high hedge and gardens, the road led to a gravelled area which had a raised garden with a group of palm trees in the middle. The house itself was also raised, with two sets of steps on either side which led to the massive front door. Later, Teresa was to learn that the path to the left led to the farm buildings and to the right led to the back door of the house, which had entrance on the ground floor.

Don Pasquale pulled the chain at the side of the door. They could hear it ringing in the house. After a while, a maid opened the door to let them in. She said to the priest that they were expected and asked if they would follow her. They passed through hallways, past many doors. How many rooms did this house have? The maid came to an impressive double door, knocked, opened it and they walked in.

'Padre Pasquale come in, come in, sit by the fire. What will you have, something hot or perhaps a drink?' Donna Beatrice smiled as she said this because she knew the answer. Although it was not yet midday, Don Pasquale would not refuse a glass of *anisetto*.

'Yes, yes that is just what I want,' he said, 'to warm the blood there is nothing like *anisetto*.' He sat down by the fire to await the maid, Rosetta, getting his drink.

Teresa was left standing. She was looking around the room and felt as if she was in a church; such a high ceiling, pictures on the walls, a huge stone fireplace and sofas large and small. On the stone floor, there was a carpet in fantastic colours.

'This is the girl, she is the daughter of Vincenzo and Matilda, the largest family in the valley.'

'Yes, I know them, I think they work some of our land and I know your Nonna Maria,' she said addressing Teresa.

Teresa stepped forward to hand the *signora* the basket. 'My nonna sends you these biscotti with her compliments.'

'Yes, put them on the table. Now, you want to work here. What can you do?' she asked.

'I can make biscotti too just like Nonna and I can sew and embroider, I went to the nuns to learn. I went to night school for only three months and can read and write.'

Just then, Rosetta walked in with a tray carrying two glasses of *anisetto* which she put down on the side table between the priest and Beatrice.

'Alright,' Donna Beatrice said to Teresa, 'you will be on trial for a month. Keep yourself clean and your clothes too, I cannot abide sloppiness. Rosetta, take her to the kitchen, tell her what her duties will be.'

Teresa remembered her mother's instructions. She curtseyed, and was about to walk away when she asked, 'May I ask how much my wage will be because my family are in dire need of it.'

Donna Beatrice was about to say that they would talk about it at the end of the month. Then she thought better of it. 'In that case, I will send the money directly to your mother every month, go now.' Teresa walked away with Rosetta, disappointed that she would not get to at least touch the money.

Don Pasquale and Donna Beatrice were left to enjoy their *anisetto* and talk of other things – a gossip is good for the soul.

CHAPTER 6

A Nun's Story

MATILDA MISSED TERESA. She was her favourite daughter, if a mother is allowed a favourite. But she loved all her children, each of them special in their own way. Teresa was special in that she was always cheerful and happy. Even when there really was nothing to be happy about, she would still be cheerful, and you could not help but be happy in her company too. Matilda really needed her to be there that day because her heart was heavy; another of her daughters was about to leave home the next morning.

Maria, her second daughter, was exactly the opposite of Teresa. Always, since she was a child, she went through life as if she carried the weight of the world on her shoulders. Then she had her first Holy Communion and things got even worse – she would be in a world of her own, often deep in thought.

Matilda would find her praying in the night. 'What are you praying for my dear?' she would ask.

She would answer, 'I am praying for you and Papà, that you will not get sick and die, for what would all of us do if you did?'

Other times, she would find her crying. 'Why are you crying my darling?' she would ask her daughter.

'Because the priest said that its all our fault that Jesus was crucified on the cross, his mother Maria, *la Madonna*, was very upset and crying at the foot of the cross.'

'That was a very long time ago, there is no need to cry now. I am sure that Our Lady, *la Madonna*, does not want you to cry and to be unhappy.'

But no amount of reassurance would get through to her. Matilda had spoken to the priest about her, and he said that some children would take the Catholicism lessons to heart, but not to worry, she would outgrow it. It came as no surprise, really, that at twelve years old she said she wanted to be a nun.

At sixteen, she said that she had a calling to serve Jesus.

At eighteen, she said that was definitely what she wanted to do, and no amount of persuasion would make her change her mind. At last, the family had to accept that was what she was going to do.

She made applications for the Holy Order. She wanted to do missionary work in Africa, to make up for the sins of the world. Matilda and Vincenzo would look at each other and raise their eyes to heaven above. She had not been accepted at any of the colleges or convents she had applied for because she had no money. College had to be paid for and convents demanded a dowry.

At last, she was offered a place in the convent near Frosinone. The order was 'Little Sisters of the Poor'.

Maria was getting ready to go, putting everything in a small suitcase. Her mother had bought her some new underwear, socks and a pair of stout shoes. She had the clothes that she was wearing, plus a change of clothes in the suitcase. She knew that once she was there, she would be given a novice habit to wear.

Was she excited to go? She did not know, the only emotion that she distinctly felt was calmness. She was fulfilling her destiny; never once had she thought of getting married and having children. She thought that all her children were waiting for her in Africa.

That night would be her last meal with her family. She would miss her grandparents, her brothers and sisters, her mamma and papà and even the little ones – she would miss them the most. Her mother gave birth to the babies and then she and her sisters would take care of them while they were little. Once they were three to four years old, the younger child would take over, watching that they did not hurt themselves while they explored the world. The mother and father were far too preoccupied in thinking on how to clothe and feed them. It had been the will of God for her mother to have so many children. Maybe it was a sin to say or even think it, that after the last was born, there would be no more, but they kept on coming, the next one due soon.

She felt guilty leaving her mother now, but she knew that there were many hands ready to take her place. It had also been the will of God for her to have this calling to the religious life.

It was time. She knew the goodbyes would be hard, but she must go. When would she see them again? Maybe in two or even three years. While she was a novice, she was not allowed visitors. Only when she had received Holy Orders would her parents be allowed to attend; after that she would be able to go within the community and to visit her family with the permission of the Mother Superior. Maria's dream was to go to

Africa: her children were waiting for her and she felt that was her destiny.

She had finished packing. She could hear Concettina calling her to eat – her last supper with her family, like Jesus, and just like Jesus this night would be her Calvary. Her heart quickened at the thought that she would leave behind everyone and everything that had been in her life until now.

In the morning she set off with her father. They walked up the track, side by side. She wanted to look back and wave a last goodbye, but she must not; from now on she would only look forward. At the high road they waited for the autobus which would take them to Sora and from there to Casamari, her destination. While they waited, Maria's friend Adelina came out of her house with her baby in her arms to wish her goodbye. They had grown up together, now one was the bride of a man and already a mother, and the other was going to be the bride of God. Adelina would never understand her friend and said a tearful goodbye when the autobus arrived. Once at her destination, and after another tearful goodbye to her father, she walked away from him to join her new family of God.

Matilda had watched her daughter until she could not see her anymore. She picked up the end of her apron to wipe her eyes, then checked herself, after all her daughter was not dead – she was going where her heart wanted to go, and as long as she was happy, then it would be fine. Yes, she said to herself, but why does my heart feel broken? This daughter of hers, since she was a baby, had pulled at her heartstrings. She had a feeling deep inside that she had failed this child, that no matter how much she had wanted her to be happy and carefree, she had never succeeded.

CHAPTER 7

A Letter from America

VINCENZO WAS OUTSIDE his house. He could see Leonardo, the postman, coming down the track. He was either coming to him or he would pass his house to go up the road to Franco's. If he was coming here, it meant only one thing – a bill to pay.

This was something new for him. He had indoor running water and electric lights installed in his house, which were fantastic commodities. But whereas before he had no bills to pay, now every three months the bills would arrive and finding the money to pay these bills was always a dilemma. Thank God there was plenty food now, after the hard time of the war. If everyone helped to work the land and the animals were properly taken care of, there was enough.

The only cash that he had was when he sold the two nine-month-old calves and some lambs, and that had to last a year. Now, for the first time, Donna Beatrice had sent Teresa's wage to his wife which would go towards the bills. His wife would sell a few eggs and that would also go towards the household expenses.

After the war their only preoccupation was having food to eat and keeping warm. The children were young – if they had enough to eat and shoes on their feet, they were happy. Now that there was no need to worry about food, they wanted so much more – what they wanted even more than clothes and shoes was a radio, but that was an impossible dream. Six of the children went to school and the expense to get them what they needed was difficult – books, jotters, their black overalls with the white collar and blue-ribbon necktie. Of course, these things would be passed on from one child to the next and some kind person would give them things that their own child no longer needed, which they were grateful to receive. Matilda would give something in return.

Vincenzo sat down in the sun to wait for the postman and rolled himself a cigarette. Every time he did this, he felt guilty. He could not break the habit and cursed the person that had invented tobacco. He went back to his review of the situation.

His son Pietro wanted to get married in September. He would be the first of his children to marry and the rest would follow. It was only natural that it was so. The good thing was that Pietro had managed to get a job at the new soap factory in Picinisco.

He could get there on foot and his mother made a packed lunch for his midday meal so he could save every lira of his wage, which would go towards his wedding. He could supply the food for the wedding feast himself. He would butcher one of his sheep, a yearling, and there were chickens, plenty of vegetables and his mother could make lasagna. His wife and her mother would bake sweet stuff. They would start to save eggs for the occasion. The eggs would be buried in deep sand in a cool place, that would keep them fresh, and there was plenty of flour. They were not destitute. He had nothing to be ashamed of.

But his thoughts turned to something he was embarrassed about, especially when he would see the smirk of amusement on the faces of his friends and relatives. His wife was due to give birth again, another child. He loved all his children and he felt bad and asked forgiveness from this unborn child that it was not wanted. He prayed to God that it would be healthy, but most of all he prayed to God that it would be the last. He had prayed for this many times, and he knew that really it was his fault. Every time, after his wife had given birth, he would say to himself, 'That is it, I am not going anywhere near her again.' He would not sleep with her, saying she needed more space in the bed with the new-born baby, and he would sleep in with his sons.

This would last a month or two, sometimes six months or longer. But Vincenzo missed her so much that he could not sleep at night. He missed her breath, her warm body next to him, her bottom tucked into his lap, her warm feet in the winter and her warm, milky smell. He missed watching her undress to come to bed, watching the child suck at her ample breast, feeling jealous of the child. He missed holding the baby in his arms to give her a rest, he missed all that and more. Then in a moment of weakness he would return to his matrimonial bed. He would see the look of amusement on the faces of his sons when they saw that their father was no longer sleeping with them.

And soon she would be expecting again. It felt as though he had only look at his wife and another baby was on the way. Why was it, he wondered? Other men enjoyed their married life and did not have so many children, eight or ten at the most, not twenty, counting the lost babies. He remembered how he and his wife mourned with hot tears when their babies had died. No matter how many children you have, you love them all. He did not mind having so many children, what ate at him was that he was not able to give them what they asked for, how they wanted what their friends had.

The postman said to him as he approached, 'You enjoying the sunshine? Soon it will be unbearable, and you will seek the shade.' Then he asked, 'When is Pietro getting married? I hear that your daughter Teresa is working as a maid at the big house... and your daughter Maria has gone away to become a nun. That must be hard to endure, and I hear that Andrea wants to emigrate...'

Vincenzo wondered if there was anything that he did not know. That is what it's like in a small town; everyone knows everything, and what they do not know they are not afraid to ask. Leonardo realised that Vincenzo was not in a talkative mood, only giving grunts for answers. He took a letter out of his satchel, gave it a good look, passed it under his nose for a sniff and handed it to Vincenzo. It wasn't a bill. It was a letter from America.

Vincenzo stared at the letter from America. He called his wife, they sat at the table and both stared at the letter, then looked at each other, a look of horror on both their faces. What news did it contain? Maybe her brother was returning and wanted his house back, or maybe he wanted to sell the house, or he wanted them to pay rent; any one of these options would be a disaster. Where would they go?

'Open it,' Vincenzo encouraged his wife.

She did as he asked. Two notes dropped out of the envelope, two fifty-dollar bills… one hundred dollars! Their looks changed to unbelieving delight.

'Here, you read it,' she said as she handed the letter to her husband. It began with, 'Dear sister and brother-in-law I hope this letter finds you well, as I am…' When Vincenzo came to the end of the letter, they stared at each other in wonder and disbelief at what Matilda's brother asked of them.

CHAPTER 8

Matilda's Baby

THE FOLLOWING DAY when the merchant came to take away the calves and lambs, he paid in cash. What a wonderful feeling it was, having that money in their pocket even when they knew that it was already spent. It had to cover so much. They loaded up the animals and the butcher was about to climb into his lorry when Vincenzo asked the merchant, as a matter of curiosity, if he had any idea how many lira you would get for a dollar.

The merchant named a figure, but he was not sure, 'Go to the bank, they would know.'

Vincenzo went into his house and, with a pencil, worked out how much one hundred dollars was worth. Matilda was there beside him. It was worth almost the same amount as the dealer had just paid for the animals. The couple decided not to tell anyone of their windfall or, before they could do anything about it, it would be spent. They would keep it for an emergency. And little did they know that an emergency was soon to happen.

That night everyone was there as usual because mealtime was not to be missed, not because their parents insisted but because of an established rule – if you were not there to eat, you would go to bed hungry. The only option was bread and cheese; before it used to be bread and onion, *cipolla*. As usual, over the meal

Vincenzo told his workforce what tasks to do the following day, and as usual Andrea was in a foul mood.

His father banged the palm of his hand on the table and shouted at his son, 'Andrea, can you tell me what's wrong with you? Every night it is the same story. I am sick of your discontent, if you are not happy do something about it, you are old enough now to find yourself a wife and get on with your life! I have had just about enough of your complaining!'

Andrea raised his voice to his father, something he rarely did because he had great respect for him, 'All right, I will tell you! I want to emigrate to Scotland.'

'Oh you do, do you? I had to hear it from the postman that you wanted to emigrate, why did you not tell me?'

'I did not tell you because wanting something and getting it are two different things! I know someone who wants to give me a job. Tony said he has work for me. He also said that I need to have five pounds, which is about fifteen thousand lira, or they will not let me into the country. Where am I going to get that kind of money? I am thinking of getting a job and saving up for it, but that would leave you in the lurch. Who will help you with the work that needs to be done on the farm?' Vincenzo's eldest son was his right-hand man and took on most of the heavy work on the land.

Vincenzo looked at his son, his anger dissipating. 'Is that really what you want to do?' He held his gaze while he said this.

'Yes, it's really what I want, I am done with the earth.'

His father looked at his wife for approval, she gave a little nod.

He took the money out of his pocket, counted out twenty thousand lira and pushed it towards his son.

'Will that do for your train ticket as well?'

Andrea pushed the money back to him, 'I can't take that, you need it, you need it for so many things. You have nothing else to sell. No, I can't take it.'

His father pushed the money back to him and said, 'You take it and let me worry about that. Go on, take it.'

The man looked at his father, as did everyone else. There was silence, with only the little ones playing on the floor as usual.

He put his hand out to take the money and put it carefully in his pocket. There were tears in his eyes. He got up and walked outside so that he could let go of the sob that was choking him.

***

They were all asleep. Matilda woke up. She had a pain in her back that she instantly recognised. She took a deep breath. 'Here we go again.' She felt tired and cuddled up to her husband. 'Please baby, wait until morning.'

Matilda had no problem giving birth after she had Pietro, her fifth child. A short labour of four to five hours and the child would come, then three days in bed and that would be it.

Her husband would tease her with affection saying that if she was a mare, she would be worth a fortune. She fell pregnant at the drop of a hat, and the child had an easy birth. She had more than enough milk for her own child and so sometimes she helped other women who, for some reason, did not have milk. She could not say no.

Even more unbelievable was that – and he could never get over his luck – she had retained her figure; a little on the plump side but he liked that, and of course, she was beautiful to him. That would never change, no matter how many wrinkles, grey hairs and double chins she got. He laughed when he said this and she would give him a push and say, 'What double chin, look at yourself!'

The pain was coming stronger now. She sat up and looked at the clock. It was four o'clock in the morning, time to get up anyway.

She nudged Vincenzo. 'Vincenzo, Vincenzo,' she said, 'the baby is coming.'

'Yes, *va bene*, just give me a minute.'

Matilda put her foot down on the tiled floor, slipped into her flip flops and lifted the little boy who was sleeping soundly beside his father. She hugged his warm little body. She carried the child into the girls' bedroom and tucked him in beside Fiorinda. She nudged Concettina to tell her that the baby was coming. Matilda's mother was already up. She was first on her feet to light the fire so that it would be warm for the little ones when they came down.

As soon as Maria saw her daughter, she told her to go back to bed. She was looking very pale. As Matilda went back to her room to await the birth of her child, she could hear the household coming to life. Concettina came to wake the twins who were sleeping in the crib and took them downstairs.

The pain was coming more frequently. Matilda's mother and Mamma Concetta were both in the room to help. Four hours had passed and there was no sign of the baby; her pain was getting unbearable. Maria was worried for her daughter.

'Vincenzo, send for the midwife, I think the baby is breech I can't see the head.'

She gave birth so easily they had stopped calling for the midwife long ago. Matilda said that just having the mothers there was enough for her. Vincenzo had insisted, but after the tenth child he had given up. His wife would get angry with him when he had to pay her.

'What!' she would say, 'She comes here to eat and drink and sleep and then we have to pay her too, your mamma and my mamma are enough for me.'

Vincenzo could hear his wife scream and his blood ran cold in his veins. Never had he heard her scream like this. His son Francesco jumped on the bike and went to fetch the midwife.

Vincenzo took the horse out of the stable, put her harness on, jumped on her and rode her hard for Picinisco to get the doctor. As he was galloping along the road, he noticed that a car was behind him. It was Mediucci in his car; he signalled him to stop. Abandoning the horse, he climbed in and told him to hurry, he had to get the doctor. Mediucci slammed his foot hard on the accelerator and the car sped away with a roar.

As soon as the doctor saw Matilda he knew that it was bad. A breech birth: she was struggling to push the baby out, but it would not budge. He knew that he had to do something, or he would lose the mother and the child.

He prepared for what he had to do, he had done it many times. A little cut would enable him to turn the infant. This was what he did, and the infant was born. A little shake made the child cry. He passed the child to the midwife and, after a quick look to see that all looked normal, she handed the baby over to his grandmother. She could see blood gushing out of Matilda.

The doctor said, 'quickly, as many rags as possible.'

The midwife took the sheet off the bed and started to rip it apart.

The doctor packed her up with the rags, but they were soon saturated. He was trying not to panic.

Then he said, 'Wrap her up in a blanket, we have to take her to the hospital.'

Vincenzo carried his wife downstairs. They got into the doctor's car and drove off, Vincenzo and her mother on each side of the sick woman.

After the car pulled away, the only sound you could hear was the crying of the newborn infant. Everyone else was in shock. How could this be happening? Concettina went to help the midwife to see to the baby. She could now hear sobs coming from downstairs.

Soon Concettina was walking up the road, a bundle in her arms. The child was crying, poor little thing, he wanted his mamma. It was about to get dark, but the house she was going to was just on the high road so she was soon there. As she walked to the door, Adelina, who had heard the cry of a baby, came out. As soon as she saw Concettina with the baby in her arms, she knew why she was there.

'Please help me, Adelina, he has been crying almost since birth. He wants his mamma.'

'Yes, come in, of course I will.'

The young woman had a baby of her own, a little four-month-old boy. She had plenty of milk, so how could she say no. She sat down and Concettina placed the child in Adelina's arms. At once, she put him to her breast. He was a big healthy boy; he was sucking greedily.

'Can I leave him with you? I have brought his things. I am so worried for my mother that I cannot think straight.' The baby had its feed and, satisfied, he fell asleep. She could see that her little brother was going to be all right.

Concettina left to go home but did not want to. She wanted to go to the hospital to see her mother. She wanted her mamma too. Up till now she had been dry-eyed, dealing with things that needed to be done. Now that she had left her baby brother safe, she was in a flood of tears. All she could see was the blood-red of the water as she had put all the bedding to soak. She stood at the turning to her house. The hospital was in Atina, not too far away. She could walk there in one hour. She set off at a brisk pace; now that she had decided to go, she wanted to get there as soon as possible. She had only walked about ten minutes when Andrea came up to her on his bike. They both knew where they were going. She sat on the handlebar of the bike in front of him and in twenty minutes they were there.

Vincenzo and his mother-in-law were in the waiting room and that was where the brother and sister found them. Matilda was in the operating room. There was nothing to do but wait and pray. After a while a nurse came dashing in. She addressed the husband, 'Your wife has lost a lot of blood. You and her mother have already given blood, is there anyone else in your family you could call on?'

Andrea and Concettina both jumped up.

'Yes, yes, we are here, she is our mother.'

'Come this way then.' They both followed her.

'There is no time for all the usual procedures. One of you come directly into the theatre room. We will put a direct line from you into your mother. Who will go first? Andrea? *Va bene*, come this way.'

When the operation was finally over, the doctor said, 'We just have to hope for the best now. The bleeding has stopped. I had to do a hysterectomy. As long as she has no more blood loss she will be alright.'

Vincenzo and his family expressed their gratitude to the doctor for saving her life.

***

It was early morning, the sun just up. It was going to be a warm day. Summer in all its full glory would soon be here.

Vincenzo was waiting for Mediucci to arrive to take him to the hospital. He was going there to bring his wife back. She had been in the hospital for two weeks and she was desperate to come home. She wanted to see her child. She kept saying to him, 'I want my baby.'

He would tell her that the baby was fine. 'You get yourself well now, stay in another couple of days until you get your strength back.' She looked so pale, as if she had no blood left in her body. The doctor said that it would take time, but she would get better.

The children could not contain their excitement; Mamma was coming home. He could not contain his excitement either; his wife was coming home. He would walk to Canneto barefoot to give thanks.

CHAPTER 9

Matilda is Feeling Blessed

MATILDA THANKED GOD that she was home to be with her baby and her other little ones. She was feeling sad that she could not breastfeed this child as she had fed all her other children. When she had come back from hospital, she had put the infant to her breast hoping that the suckling would stimulate her breasts to produce milk. The little boy was so frustrated that he screamed. With a tear in her eye, she had to face the fact that she would not be able to suckle this one.

Her mother, Mamma Concetta and Papà Andrea were glad when she eventually gave up. She needed all her resources for herself, to put colour back in her cheeks.

Her recovery was slow; she moved about the house very carefully, she had to stop often to rest. She was not able to do all the things she had done before. This frustrated her, but her family reassured her that there were many hands to do what needed to be done. It became Stefania's job to take the baby back and forth each day to Adelina to be fed. It became Antonio and Giuseppe's job to go every day to the butcher to buy one hundred grams of beef fillet or liver. Both were said to make blood in the body. Matilda was getting better. At least, she felt that her body was recovering from her ordeal. What was holding her back from being herself again was that she had things on her mind which were troubling her. She worried about her daughter Maria, knowing that she was not that far away, yet she could not go to see her. She wished that Maria could write to her. Matilda had written a few times to the Mother Superior asking how Maria was. She had not received a reply. All she could see in front of her eyes was Maria's sad face as she walked away from home.

Andrea had left for *La Scozia* a few weeks ago. She and his father had to persuade him not to change his plans at the last minute because of his mother's illness. He wanted to return the money, saying that they needed it now, even more than before. Medical bills had to be paid. Where would they get the money? At length they had to tell him about the money that his uncle had sent from America. The medical bills had been paid.

Eventually, he agreed to go, reassuring his father that as soon as he had earned a little money he would send it to him.

With a small cardboard case, he began his journey to that far off land that was swallowing all the best young people of this land. It had been a sad, heart-wrenching goodbye.

'It's not forever Mamma, I will be back,' he had said to her as he climbed in the taxi he was sharing with another young man leaving the mother country.

After his departure there was a void in her heart. He had a special place there. Her first child, she had him when she was a child herself. They had grown up together.

She knew she had to shake herself out of her sadness for the sake of the others. In September, Pietro was getting married to Anna. There were things to do, plans to make. He was the first child to marry, it was a milestone in her life, and it should be and would be a happy occasion. At the back of her mind was also that letter from America. She must at least write back to her brother, thanking him for the money and telling him how it had been a Godsend.

The other things that he had said in his letter, she could not address now, but they were thinking about it.

Matilda called her daughters. She said to them, 'I want to have a bath, a proper bath, not just a wash. I want to immerse my whole body in warm water, to wash away my illness, that horrible smell of the hospital, and give my mind a good clean too. I have been miserable for too long. Help me to get that old tin bath that is in the hay loft, put more wood on the fire and get a good flame to heat the water.'

The sheer luxury to lie in the warm water! Her hair was squeaky clean and she had put some dried lavender in the bath water. She just lay there until the water turned cold. Then she got out to dress, ready for the family coming home.

That evening she felt like a new woman. The first to notice how well she looked was her husband. He stopped and stared at her, for a brief moment he saw her as his bride from long ago.

When it was time for bed, in passing, Matilda whispered in his ear, 'Come and sleep with me tonight.'

Vincenzo had not slept with his wife since her return from hospital because she had the baby, Lorenzo, with her in bed, and also because of her delicate health. She did not have to say it twice. He followed her up the stairs. Vincenzo was quick to undress and get into the bed, ready for his first pleasure. He loved to watch her undress. She lifted the baby from the bed and put him with his brother in the crib.

Then she let down her hair giving it a good shake and scratch. She smiled to herself. She knew how much he was enjoying it. But she did it naturally, as she did every night. She put her foot on the chair, she removed her stocking, unbuttoned her skirt and let it fall on the floor. She picked it up, gave it a good shake and put it on the back of the chair. Finally, she unbuttoned her blouse and slipped it off. She turned the light off. She did it all slowly as if she was alone in the room. Then she climbed into the bed when the pretence was over, and she laughed.

He made love to her slowly, carefully, as he did not want to hurt her. It was almost like their wedding night when they were young and carefree. He held her in the crook of his arm, gently stroking her. For the first time in a long time, he was at peace. He had his wife in his arms, he had made love to her and did not feel worried; there would be no more babies. Feeling guilty for thinking that, he quickly said to himself, 'Thank you Lord for all of my healthy children. I have been blessed.'

CHAPTER 10

Teresa

TERESA HAD BEEN at the *palazzo* for two months. She had quickly learned her duties in the house. She was a fast learner; they only had to tell her once. One month ago, she was told she would be waiting at the table. It was a good distance from the kitchen to the dining room; it was a job the more experienced servants would rather not do, so they were happy for the new girl to do it.

Teresa did not mind. She liked the new clothes she was given to wear, so that she would look smart. She also liked the topics discussed at the table between the parents and their sons, Gian Filippo, the youngest at thirty-nine years old, Felice and Stefano, and any guests that were invited for dinner. The girl was getting quite good at the job, giving no indication at all that she was listening: no eye contact, standing aside when she was not needed and looking straight ahead.

She loved the *palazzo* now that she knew most of the rooms. She cleaned the bedrooms every day. When she cleaned the grand salon, Teresa would close her eyes and hold her arms up to waltz round and round with her imaginary partner. It was a beautiful room, with frescoes on the walls and seating all around, the sofas in vibrant colours.

Rosetta said that the salon was used when the sons were young. They used it for balls, parties at Christmas and Easter and birthday parties. There was also a smaller but equally beautiful room which was used whenever they had visitors and a living room which the family used every day. Then there was the large dining room which was also used every day. The table was small for the size of the room. Rosetta said that there was another table which was added when needed.

Teresa would walk briskly through the house, head up, shoulders back. She would imagine that she was the daughter of the house. Wearing beautiful, flowing silk dresses, high-heeled shoes and her hair cut into a modern bob, she would have friends to visit, friends she had met at college in Rome. Young and handsome boys would come just to court her.

She had a fantastic imagination and always had a story going on in her head. She would put the story aside if she was in the kitchen with the others, but as soon as she was alone, cleaning, making the beds or setting the table, she would go back to it.

The young girl had just started a new story. It had taken just one glance for the story to begin.

She had been serving at the table as usual and was being very careful not to spill anything. After all, she did not want to be demoted back to the kitchen.

She was serving soup, totally engrossed in being careful. She had just served Gian Filippo and was about to fill the bowl of his brother Felice.

'Ouch, that was hot!'

Gian Filippo had overturned the soup onto his lap. She quickly put the soup tureen on the sideboard and went to help him with napkins to clean up. As she was doing this, she looked up to meet his eyes. He was staring at her. Their eyes met for a moment before she walked away to continue with her duties. That was when the story in her head started. He was twenty years younger; she was seventeen. He was dashing and funny. He loved to sing and dance. He would wear white silk shirts tucked into his riding breeches and black leather boots that reached as far as his knees.

She was only a servant, but she was bewitching with flashing eyes and flaming red hair. She was irresistible and so the story went. Now this story, which was only a fantasy, put ideas in her head which were not there before. For the last two months she had remembered what her mother had said to her, and every time she passed the three brothers she kept her eyes down and walked on unless she was asked to do something. This had not been difficult because she had found them unattractive and old. Ever since they had exchanged that look at the table, whenever she came into contact with Gian Filippo, and if they were alone, he would look at her and she would give him a quick glance and a smile.

She was a very attractive girl; he would return the smile and his eyes would follow her. It became kind of flirtation, but only their eyes were involved.

Teresa, after a while, would not see Gian Filippo as he really was. Forty years old, grey hair and greying beard. He walked in a peculiar way, one arm swinging at his side. She began to see him as he was in her story. She was young, only seventeen; she did anything to make her life more exciting.

On Sunday, after she had served the Sunday *pranzo*,

lunch, she was allowed to go home for the afternoon. It was a time she really enjoyed – seeing her family, especially her siblings.

It became a habit that on her way back to work at the *palazzo* Gian Filippo, who 'happened' to be passing in his car, would give her a lift. She would sit in the back seat in silence. Then one day he asked her to sit at the front, and they began to exchange a few words.

It must be said that she did all the talking. She was a bright girl, vivacious, and although her education had been minimal, she could talk about anything. He, on the other hand, despite having had a good education in Rome and many life experiences, was very dull. His speech was slow, and he did not have much sense of humour. He found the girl fascinating. Her sparkle and laughter, which she tried to suppress because she didn't think it would be appropriate to laugh in his presence. After all, he was *il padrone*.

The Tarttaglia family were not always at home. Though Donna Beatrice was at an age where she did not enjoy travelling and her husband, who was many years older than herself, enjoyed it even less, one thing that they had not given up was going to the seaside for the month of July. The doctor said it was a must because the sea air was good for their bones. It would do them a world of good. They had a villa in Gaeta. Donna Beatrice would send two maids beforehand to clean the villa, to get everything ready before she and her husband would follow.

It was agreed that Angelica (the cook), Rosetta and Teresa would go. One of the girls would come back once everything was done; after all, two staff in attendance was enough for an elderly couple.

Donna Beatrice wrote a note to Teresa's mother to inform her of their plan.

Matilda was not happy about this and was beginning to regret letting Teresa go to the *palazzo* to work. She felt as if she had no choice but to agree not to offend *la signora* and how could they stop Teresa – she wanted to go. She wrote back giving her consent.

After a few days of preparations, the car was loaded with food and other things that the couple could not do without. Gian Filippo would drive the girls to Gaeta, open the house and then leave for Rome where the family had property that needed to be seen to. On his way back he would pick up one of the girls to take her home.

Teresa really enjoyed being in Gaeta. Rosetta had been before and showed her around. The villa was situated in the bay of Gaeta, not far from the sea. The beach was full of children playing on the sand. Anyone who could afford it would take their children to the seaside for a month, and families who did not have a villa would rent an apartment. The mothers would come with the nanny for the children. The husband would come for the weekend, then back for business on Monday.

The air worked wonders for the children and for the people of a certain age like Donna Beatrice and her husband.

Teresa thought it worked wonders for the young people too. They had so much fun strolling on the promenade with like-minded people, boys and girls. Many heads turned to admire the two girls. Angelica, who sometimes walked with them, noticed the turning heads and she also noticed the encouragement they had from Teresa.

By the end of the week, the villa was clean from top to bottom; the windows and green shutters were clean, the garden tidied up, the garden furniture washed and set out in front of the house on the patio where you could sit and watch the passers-by. The balconies had a few potted plants which Angelica had bought at the market. It was nice to sit there; you could see the sea. While this was only for the family, Teresa would enjoy the view when she was cleaning.

It was Friday. Teresa had been to the market. The market was only a few minutes' walk from the villa. She went to buy some fresh produce, vegetables and fruit. She loved walking along the rows of stalls selling everything from food to clothes, flowers and of course, being by the seaside, fish. Teresa would look and look at the fish – there were so many different kinds, many she did not even know the name of. Some of the produce was not called fish but *frutto di mare*, fruit of the sea. She would ask *la signora* if one day she could cook *spaghetti alle vongole*, pasta with clams for them, which she already knew how to make. She finished buying what she needed and went to prepare for the family's arrival that night.

It was July – Gaeta at night was buzzing. There were outdoor concerts to enjoy. Many visitors came to see La Roccia Spagata. Others came to visit family members who were in prison. Gaeta had the biggest prison in the area. There was also a castle, a fortress on the highest prominence on the peninsula.

Teresa loved it, she had never seen anything like it. The tree-lined streets. The palm-lined promenade. Flowers everywhere, beautiful flowers, not just the wildflowers she was used to. Even the garden of the estate in Picinisco did not have such flowers. There was one flower especially, bougainvillea, that was everywhere, on buildings, climbing trees; it came in four colours, magenta, pink, peach and creamy white.

The women were also a pretty sight, elegant in colourful summer dresses, sleeveless with deep necklines. Some wore straw hats, others had parasols to protect their complexion from the sun.

The sun was fierce and made the air shimmer and sparkle over the sea. When she had first seen the sea, she was frightened; such a massive amount of water, surely it would come in and drown them all. But then she had seen the waves break on the beach and was reassured that it would not come any further.

Late in the afternoon, Donna Beatrice and her husband arrived. Teresa was sent upstairs to unpack their luggage and put everything away in their wardrobe and dresser. As she walked down the stairs, she overheard Angelica speaking with *la signora*.

'It's best that Rosetta stays, the other is troublesome.'

'Yes, I have noticed that too,' said the lady of the house.

Just then, Gian Filippo walked in. Teresa could not help smiling at him. 'Welcome back, *signorino*,' she said as she took his hat.

The next day, after the midday meal was over and the kitchen cleaned, Angelica told Teresa that she was going back to the *paese* and to get her things ready to go. Teresa was expecting this after what she had overheard the day before. She was really disappointed; she would have liked to stay. But she did as she was told and soon after she climbed into the back seat of the car. After ten minutes Gian Filippo stopped the car and asked her to sit in the front.

CHAPTER 11

Smallpox

THE SUN WAS SHINING as it did day after day. The light changed from the clear, fresh and energising rays of the early morning to the hazy stillness of the afternoon. Then, in late afternoon, the romantic, rosy glow. Night came all at once, with all its own splendour: the crickets would sing, the frogs would croak and the dogs would bay at the moon as they roamed the countryside in a pack looking for romance.

It was on a morning such as this, the Valente family were each busy in their own occupation. The three little ones, Lia, Erica and Bruno, were sitting on the floor in a corner of the kitchen. They knew better than to sit in the middle of the floor where more than once they had been stood on or knocked over. Each child had a tin plate in front of them that held bread soaked with the whey from the cheesemaking that had bits of ricotta floating in it and a little sugar on top – that was their breakfast. They ate big spoonfuls and soon it was finished. The children put the plates and spoons on the table and were about to go out to play when their mother called them.

'Lia, Erica, Bruno, come here.'

The children pretended not to hear and went out.

'Stefania... would you get the little ones before they disappear? I have to get them washed.'

'Why is it always Stefania, could you call someone

else?' replied the girl. She was in her whiny mood. She went to fetch the children.

'Did you not hear Mamma calling you? Come inside, Mamma wants you.'

Stefania picked up Bruno and pushed the twin girls back inside the house. She sat the boy on the table and was about to go away.

'Stefania, don't go away, help me take their clothes off.'

'Stefania'... again, thought the girl.

When the three children were bathed, it was 'Stefania, would you go upstairs, look through the baskets and find some clean and half-decent clothes for them?' The petulant girl did as she was told. She came down with an armful of clothes in an assortment of colours. Matilda then went to get herself ready.

'Stefania, watch the children. Make sure they don't go outside, they will get dirty.'

'Oh Mamma! Stefania, Stefania... is there nobody but me in this house? You watch them, Nonna, I am going upstairs to get ready too.'

Vincenzo had Bruno in his arms, Matilda was holding Lia and Erica by their hands, and Stefania walked along beside them. They were soon at the high road in front of Adelina's house. They stood in line to wait for the autobus to take them to Picinisco, but they were not the only ones there. There was a crowd of people and many children. The autobus soon came, it was almost full already, and everyone pushed to get on the bus. Vincenzo was pushing the hardest, but still there was no more space.

Vincenzo held the door of the bus open and he shouted inside, 'Look, my wife has just come out of hospital, she has had a big operation and she needs a seat on this autobus. Someone give her a seat.

'You there,' he said to a young man, 'give her your seat you can walk.'

The boy was put on the spot; he had no choice but to give up his seat. Matilda sat down with Bruno on her lap. With a roar from the engine, straining with its heavy load, the bus set off on the uphill, winding road to Picinisco.

Vincenzo said to his daughter, 'We will walk, there is no point waiting for another bus, it will also be full.'

They set off on their way, each holding a bewildered little girl by the hand. Vincenzo went to the youth who had given up his seat on the bus, slapped him on the back and pulled the boy to him.

'Come, you can walk with us. I know so many shortcuts that we will be there before the bus. What is your name?' he asked the shy boy.

'Matteo,' he replied.

'Matteo, this is Stefania, Lia and Erica, my three daughters, but if none of these are to your liking, I have five more at home,' and with a roar of laughter they were on their way.

Stefania looked on, amused. Maybe today would be fun after all.

It was a steep climb to Picinisco, but soon they were there. The *piazza* was full of people. The children by far outnumbered the adults. It was like a feast day. Vincenzo was looking for his wife, but in such a mass of people how would he find her? He held on tight to the twin girls. Stefania had already disappeared. He pushed his way through the throng when, at last, he could see a mass of people standing in a line, his wife queueing with all the other folk, Bruno in her arms.

He made his way to her, took the child from his wife and said, 'Take the girls, see if you can find somewhere to sit. I will stand in line with Bruno.' Vincenzo was one of the few men standing in line because it was assumed only women would have the patience to do so. The men were standing in groups talking, drinking, passing the time of the day.

The line moved slowly, but at least it moved. Vincenzo could see Stefania with some other youngsters having a good time. He called her over. 'Stefania, look for your mother, help her with the girls and don't disappear because once it's our turn, you have to call your mother to bring Lia and Erica. Do you understand what I am saying, this is no time for playing,' he said to her in a stern voice.

She walked away to look for her mother. Why is it always me? Do this, do that… she had been having fun with Matteo, her new friend.

Finally, it was nearly their turn. Matilda, Stefania and the girls made their way to the front of the line where Vincenzo was with Bruno. There were about five families in front of them. At the top of the line there was an uproar, parents instructing and consoling children, little boys and girls crying, sobbing into their parents' breasts. Bigger children howled out loud, some saying that they did not want it and trying to run away, their fathers holding them down.

Vincenzo and Matilda looked on. It had to be done, they had no choice! They held in their hands the birth certificates of the three little ones; it was their turn to get the smallpox vaccination. By law, all children had to have this vaccine. There was a stiff fine if parents failed to bring their children to be vaccinated.

They each had a child to comfort on their way home.

CHAPTER 12

The Boys

IT WAS SUMMER. For the family, life went on as usual. Work was done in season and Vincenzo made sure it was done to the best of each person's ability. The heat, especially during the day, was unbearable so most of the work was done in early morning and late afternoon.

There was time for a nap in the hottest part of the day; all very well for some, but not for others. Pietro would go to see his girl at every opportunity although it was a long walk to Fontitune. Francesco would also go to see Catarina. She could not get enough of him. Sometimes Francesco would go to the bar, sit outside on the *terrazza* to nurse a beer and to be with his friends. Catarina would see him and she would go in a sulk, go on and on about him not loving her, preferring to be with his friends instead of her. She was even worse if she saw him talking to a girl; then it would be quarrels, tears and tantrums. Francesco was fed up with her behaviour; she was just too full on with him, too clingy and jealous.

Francesco had had a letter from his brother Andrea. In the letter there was some money, ten shillings. He said it was enough for a few beers. It was a long letter telling Francesco all about his life in Edinburgh. At the bottom it said, 'You should come here too brother. Maybe if we both worked and saved, we could buy a business together. There are many opportunities here and when you have worked the four-year contract you are free to do as you please.'

The younger boys were also in no mood to nap – napping was for old folk.

Giovanni, who was twelve, and his ten-year-old twin brothers, Antonio and Giuseppe, would wander about calling on friends and waiting to see what opportunities came their way.

One of their favourite things to do was steal fruit. They would gang up with the other boys. They knew when the fruit trees were ready for picking.

Of course, there were some trees that were easy targets, in a field on their own, where no one could see you. But the best trees, orange, cherry, pear and kaki, were usually close to the houses.

The best time to try your luck was at siesta time. They had a plan on how to do this. A boy would climb the tree, another would catch the fruit as he threw it down, another would keep watch and, if the owner happened to come by, he would distract him, giving the others time to run away with the loot.

On very hot days like today, they would go to Mallarino, a river that acted as the boundary between the *comune*, the councils, of Picinisco and Villa Latina. The boys of both towns had created a pool over the years. They would strip off and dive in.

If other things came their way, how could they refuse? If, on their wanderings, they came across a lone chicken that had strayed from home, a well-calculated aim with a stone would knock the bird down and they would finish it off by wringing its neck. Then with a penknife they would remove the skin, feathers and all; it was too much trouble to take off the feathers first. A fire was lit, then roast chicken for everyone. They did not consider this stealing; it was the chicken's fault. It had wandered off and if they did not eat it, surely a fox would.

The highlight of their thieving came at the *festa*; every little town would have a feast for their patron saint. People made their living by putting up stalls to sell roasted peanuts, toys for children, ice cream and huge piles of watermelons. The boys were experts on stealing watermelons. One boy would watch for when the seller was busy selling a melon to a family – usually this took more time and effort. The wife would look at one melon then another, not able to make up her mind, continually tapping the melon like a drum to see if it made the right sound for ripeness. The children also had their say; they wanted it bigger. The vendor would be distracted.

The smallest boy of the gang, who looked young and innocent, would casually go near the pile of fruit. He had already been told by one of the bigger boys which melon he had to go for: one at the edge on its own that would not bring the pile crashing down when he moved it.

Then, he would back-kick the melon to another boy, who would casually kick it to the next, who would pick it up and calmly walk away with it and no one would know that a melon had been stolen. But sometimes they would be caught out and they would have to make a run for it.

One other thing that the band of like-minded boys

liked to do was very lucrative for them: it was to roam around the countryside, hills and woods looking for scrap metal. All that area had scrap metal, but in the fields that had been cultivated the metal had already been lifted, so the boys had to go further afield. You never knew where you would find the iron nuggets. The boys wandered about, sometimes finding wild asparagus on their travels which they would bring to their mothers to make a frittata.

The scrap metal was shrapnel from bombs, firearms and landmines. This area had been on the frontline of the war. The Battle of Monte Cassino had been fought for six months; the Allied army against the Germans. Many people lost their lives, soldiers on both sides and many civilians. Some of the older boys remembered it well.

As soon as they had a cache of metal, they would bring the scrap to a merchant who would give them money, yes, real money, to do with as they pleased.

Giovanni had a few coins in his pocket and he had plans for them.

The boys were lying on the grassy area at the edge of the pool, naked, drying off. Boys doing what boys do. Giovanni said, 'I could eat some fruit, what about you!'

The following day, Giovanni and his brother Osvaldo were walking home. It was hay making time and they had been to a field, turning over the rows of grass which had been cut the day before. As they walked along, the rakes over their shoulders, Giovanni was jiggling the few coins in his pocket.

He asked his older brother, who was sixteen,

'Osvaldo, have you been with a woman, you know, properly, all the way?'

He knew it was unlikely, but not impossible. If you knew whom to ask, there was an underground fund of knowledge as to which girl would go some of the way, and who would go all the way. He himself knew a girl that would go some of the way if you gave her a few coins, and he had heard of other boys that had been with a woman that would let you do whatever you wanted. This was a woman whose husband had gone to America and had never returned, although he would send money home. This woman did it for her own pleasure, or so the underground gossip went. The gossip also said that she was not a pretty sight; although she was only about thirty-five, she looked old and wrinkled.

Osvaldo thought for a moment, looked at his brother and said, 'Of course, I have been with a woman many times.'

'Tell me about it, what was it like?' asked Giovanni.

'You're too young to be thinking about all that, let's talk about something else.'

Giovanni thought that his brother was strange, what is there that is more interesting than 'fucking'?

He went on to say, 'I know this girl who won't let you go all the way, but she lets you do just about everything else. Why don't you come with me, I think I have enough money for us both.'

Osvaldo turned around as he said, 'No, I have to go home to study, you know I have an exam soon.'

'Yes, but it won't take long, and you can study later, you should really let yourself go a little, you are always shut away with your books.'

Giovanni could not understand him. Yes, he did have to study, but Osvaldo was the cleverest of all the children. In fact, Don Pasquale had arranged for Osvaldo to take an exam for a bursary, and if he passed the examination he would be accepted to a school in Sora for gifted children. It was run by the archdiocese and the teachers were mostly priests. It was a widely renowned elite school.

Giovanni was glad that he was not gifted. He would go where he wanted to go on his own; he jiggled the coins in his pocket.

CHAPTER 13

Osvaldo

OSVALDO DID HAVE a girlfriend. She was a year younger – they had been childhood sweethearts. For the last four years, it was known that she was his *sposa*, his girl. They walked to school together and back again, either she would look for him or he would look for her.

They would talk quietly about this or that. He would carry her books, and when it came to the turning to her house, he would hand the books to her and say, 'I will see you tomorrow then,' wait until she walked away and then go home.

A couple of years ago he had tried to kiss her, but she had pulled away, saying that she was not that kind of girl. Her mother had told her that she was not allowed to kiss any boys until she was engaged. He had not tried to kiss her again, but he felt that he should. Maybe he could start with just a kiss on her cheek. He was feeling a little foolish, to have a girl for four years and he had not kissed her. Tomorrow she was coming to his house. One day a week she came to get some help with her schoolwork. This would be his last year at school. If he passed the exam he was studying for, he would go to college in Sora. If he did not pass the exam, that would be it, his education would be over. But he was quite confident that he would pass.

He thought that before he left for college, he would have no choice but to kiss her.

Osvaldo and Lisa were sitting on a makeshift seat, a bale of hay, and they had also rigged up a sort of table at which they studied. It was the only place they could get some peace to do their lessons. Lisa wanted to do well at school, she wanted to go to a teacher training college. Osvaldo had been a great help to her. He was so clever, everything came easy to him. He was always the first in his class. They were sitting close together as he explained a maths problem to her. When he turned to look at her while she was writing something in her notebook, he looked at her closely. He had not really looked at her for a long while, she was just always there. She was just Lisa.

He noticed that she was pink, blushing with a fine shine of moisture, and her brow and upper lip had actual beads of sweat. He wondered why this was; it was not that hot. He could see the beat of her pulse on her throat.

He took a deep breath and kissed her on the cheek. He could almost hear her heart pumping away in her chest. She turned to him.

The next thing her lips were stuck on his, her mouth open, engulfing all his mouth, her arms around his neck pulling him to her. He had to push her away, he was choking. He pulled away from her and held her at arm's length. They looked into each other's eyes and neither liked what they saw. Lisa lowered her eyes with embarrassment. All at once she stood up, grabbed her things, pushed them into her bag and left, not looking back.

Osvaldo did not stop her. He was in shock – this was a side of her that he had not seen before. The look in her eyes was of pure hunger and that hunger was for him. Was it possible that it had always been there, and he had not seen it? Was it something new? Perhaps when he saw her tomorrow, she would be her old self. He would have to be patient with her. Tomorrow she would feel ashamed, perhaps she would say that she was sorry, and they would go back to the way things were. He sat for a while, deep in thought. Was it perhaps him, was he to blame for her reaction? Perhaps he should not have kissed her without asking her first.

After a while, he was still sitting in the hay loft, still thinking about whether it was his fault. Maybe he should have responded to her in the way she had to him, but he had too much respect for her. Still in thought, he looked at his hands, he listened to his heart, his breathing. They were all normal. He did not have any of the uncontrollable emotions that she had.

Tomorrow he would talk to her, they would talk about this, like they talked about everything. Then everything would be all right.

The following morning, he walked to the turning for her house and waited for her as he did every morning. She was late. If she was not there soon, they would be late for school. He wondered if she was all right, if should he run up to the house to ask. He did not know what to do, this had never happened before. Then he thought she must be feeling too upset about what had happened. He decided to be extra nice to her, as if nothing had happened. He decided to go to school even though he was very late.

After school, Osvaldo waited at the usual place for

her. Then he asked a classmate of Lisa's if she had been to school that day. Yes, she had, she had left to go home with one of her friends. Osvaldo was troubled now. He walked home alone. Far ahead in the distance he could see Lisa.

Should he run and catch up with her? But she was with her friends and he did not want to speak to her in front of them.

He would speak with her tomorrow. He was sure that by tomorrow she would be her normal self.

That tomorrow never came. She had finished with him and avoided him at all times.

He felt a loneliness he had never felt before. He had lost his best friend. His life had had a certain routine and it was not easy for him to replace her as his time had been spent mostly with her and he did not have many friends.

He kept going over what had happened in his mind and the more he thought about it, the more he blamed himself. Had his response to her been all wrong? Should he have thrown her on the straw and ravaged her, was that what she had wanted? But at the time he had felt a repulsion for her; the heat in her made him turn to ice. At night he could not sleep. He did not want to go to school. He felt that school did not have anything more to teach him.

One day he went to see Don Pasquale. He told him that he was ready to take his exam for the bursary and asked could he arrange it with the episcopal *curia* in Sora. Once he had been to see the priest to arrange his exam, he put all the thoughts aside. He went over and over all the work he had done, he revised and learned everything by heart until he thought he could do no more.

Then he relaxed, helped about the house, had long talks with Nonno Andrea and played with the little ones until, at last, he could put all that behind him and look forward to his new adventure, learning new things that he loved. Maybe one day he would be a professor and make his folks, all of them, proud of him.

CHAPTER 14

She Wanted to be Dead

TERESA HAD ENJOYED her trip to Gaeta so much. She had liked everything. The villa, the sea, all the people who were there to enjoy themselves. They were so different from the community she knew, her own family and the people that lived in the towns. Before she had thought that the people that lived in the towns were sophisticated. Now she could see that really, they were nothing special.

Needless to say, her imagination now had a much bigger scope for fantasy. In the house, there was only Gian Filippo. His brothers were away from home. They had joined friends who were having a house party in Roccaraso, a skiing resort in the Abruzzi mountains. The chalet in the mountains was also used for summer sports. The girl had time to sit and dream, and dream she did! In the garden, sitting at the kitchen table, while making the bed and even when she was waiting at the table. Gian Filippo was not much of a talker. Sometimes not even one word passed between them. But she would notice that his eyes followed her. She smiled to herself. After all, what woman does not like to be admired?

It was Sunday. Teresa spent her free afternoon with her family. She was on the way back to the *palazzo*, and as usual Gian Filippo just 'happened' to be passing. He stopped the car to let her climb in. By now she sat at the front, not waiting to be invited.

At the house she walked around the property to

enter by the back door. She went in the kitchen, looked to see what there was to be done. She was alone; the cook who was standing in for Angelica was not in the house. Then she remembered that this morning Gian Filippo had risen from his bed very late, and she had not cleaned his room. Humming to herself she went to the cupboard to get what she needed and walked up the stairs. She knocked on his door. No answer. She opened the door and walked in. She began with the bed, took all the bedding, opened the door to the balcony and gave everything a good shake over the railing. After, she remade the bed, all nice and neat and fresh.

Just then Gian Filippo walked in and was surprised to see her. Teresa said she was sorry that she was there, she would leave and come back later.

'No,' he said, 'just carry on, you are here now.'

She thought to herself, the bed is made, just a quick dusting and I will go. I will leave the floor for tomorrow.

Gian Filippo sat at his desk and seemed busy with some papers.

When she was finished, she was about to go when as she passed him, he sprung up and held her arm.

'Don't go yet,' he said.

'I am finished.'

'Yes, but stay a while.'

'I am sorry, but I can't stay, I have so much to do. Let go of my arm… please.'

'Give me a kiss first,' he smiled at her.

'Sir, that would not be appropriate.'

'Come on, you know you want to.'

'Let go of my arm now or I will scream.'

'Who do you think will hear you?'

Teresa remembered the cook was not in the house. She pulled her arm away, wanting to go, but he held her tight, now with both arms. He was trying to kiss her.

She struggled, but he was so much stronger. Then he pushed her onto the bed where he overpowered her, and no one heard her scream.

He lay there panting beside her. She lay with her eyes shut; she did not want to open them. She wanted to be dead.

She sat up, opened her eyes, looked at herself, her clothes ripped apart. She realised that she was bare and quickly covered herself with her bloodstained skirt.

He was still there beside her. She felt an uncontrollable anger towards him and started to pound him with her fists.

'Look at what you have done! Look at me, look at what you have done!' She pulled her skirt up to show him her bloody thighs.

'You have ruined me, how am I going to explain this to my future husband? How will I tell my mother? My father and brothers will kill you… you are a monster!' The girl adjusted herself to go. She wanted to run all the way home.

Gian Filippo also stood up, 'Don't go please, I am sorry, I do not know what came over me. Let's talk about it, don't go now, think about it, nobody needs to know.'

'No one needs to know?' she shouted. 'But I am going to tell your parents, and I am going to tell my parents and I am going to tell the *carabinieri*, the police. Fuck you, I am going to tell everyone that you took my honour by force, that you took advantage of a seventeen-year-old girl that was under your protection and your roof. And you call yourself an honourable man!'

'Teresa, please don't do that, think about it first, there is shame for you as well as me. I will make it up to you, let's talk about it tomorrow.'

Teresa stormed out of the room. She was now glad that there was no one at home. She ran to her room to see to herself and pack her bag to go home.

She lay on the bed and cried. She could see the reaction on the faces of her family when she walked in. She could hear the voice of the gossips. She would be known as the girl who was raped by the *signore* on the hill.

She looked at herself in the mirror. She looked the same, there was no outward sign on her face of what had happened. How could that be when inside she felt like a completely different person? Then she lay without moving; her well-developed imagination was looking at what her life would be like. She thought about it all night, a sleepless night. Perhaps it was better to keep quiet and not tell anyone.

In the morning she went about her work as if nothing had happened. Later, she would speak to Gian Filippo and see what he had to say for himself. It was late morning before she saw him. She was in the dining room setting the table when he walked in with his peculiar one-sided walk, one arm swinging at his side. It was even more pronounced than usual. As he stood there, she saw him as he really was, no longer as she had seen him in her fantasy. He could not meet her eye. Looking in the distance, over her shoulder, he stammered. He did not know how to start.

'Teresa, I am really sorry about what happened. I promise I will never do such a terrible thing again. I am truly ashamed of myself. It's something I have never done before, I am not a bad person, I do not know what came over me. I will make it up to you. I have been awake all night thinking of how I could do this. I know you would feel insulted if I offered you money, so I am not going to do that. I am going to Rome now. We will talk about it when I come back. Please don't say anything to anyone because it will not do any good for you... or for me.'

He walked to the door, then turned back. This time he looked at her and was about to say something else but stayed silent and walked away. Teresa could hear his car drive off.

Teresa pulled out one of the dining chairs and sat down. She put her hands to her face to shut out everything. What was she to do? She wanted to go home, she needed her mother's arms around her. She wanted to confide about her ordeal to her Nonna Maria. She kept saying to herself that tomorrow she would go home, pack her few things and go home.

It was not until Sunday that she went and she did not bring her bag. She set off early in the morning so she could spend all day with them. Vincenzo was surprised to see her arrive so early. His wife and most of the women were not at home, they had gone to Picinisco for Sunday mass.

As she walked into the house, he asked why she

had got all day off work. She told him that the family were away from home, so there was not much to do. Vincenzo asked, 'Are you well? You look upset about something, are you alright?'

She reassured him that she was fine and asked him what there was to be done. Then she said, 'I will prepare the *sugo*, sauce, for the family, so they will find it ready when they come back,' and she got going with that. It was better than standing about. Her father, she knew, would soon get it out of her, that everything was not fine.

She got a large aluminium pot – everything in that house was extra-large – and put it on the pepi-pepi gas. This was something new, a two-ringed gas cooker on a stand which housed a Calor gas canister. This was a great help because although all large pots of soup, polenta and pasta were still cooked on the open fire, smaller things like *sugo* for pasta, frying eggs, tossing vegetables, making frittata and so on were done on this small cooker. It was very useful and clean to use.

Teresa got all the ingredients ready for the Sunday *sugo*. She walked to the *dispensa*, the storeroom. There were shelves full of *passata* which was made last year. Soon they would be making this year's tomato *passata*. There were shelves of pickled vegetables of every kind, vegetables preserved in *olio*.

Hanging from the ceiling were the remains of the pig from last year. There was *prosciutto*, parma ham, *ventresca*, pork belly, *lardo*, lard and *strutto*, balls of melted fat which had been poured into the pig bladder, then solidified. There were just a few sausages left in a steel bin.

Also in the corner, kept just off the floor, was a heap of potatoes well covered so no light would get to them to turn them green.

Then there was a sack each of wheat flour, polenta flour, beans and chickpeas, a steel bin full of extra virgin oil, preserved olives ready to eat and another bin with pears preserved in water and salt.

This was all their own produce, but it had to last a year, until their next harvest. One thing you did not see in the storeroom was wine; their land had to produce all the essentials, so they could not use it to produce wine. Sometimes if there was a surplus Vincenzo would barter for wine with his friend Giacomo, Adelina's father.

Teresa took what she needed: a slice of pork belly, a slab of lard, a scoop of pork fat, a head of garlic, three onions and four large jars of *passata*.

She then wandered out to the *orto*, the vegetable garden, to get a bunch of parsley and basil and, since there were plenty, some ripe cherry tomatoes. She made a scoop with her apron and filled it with the tomatoes to add whole to the *sugo* about half an hour before it was ready. It gave the *sugo* extra sweetness.

It was simply done. She put the *battilardo*, the chopping board, on the table. It was ancient, a thick slice of wood, old and sealed with fat, and an equally old wooden mallet which was flat at one side and wedged on the other. On the *pista lardo* she put the lard, parsley, herbs and garlic and beat them with the mallet until they made a rough paste. She put it in the pot to *sorfrige*, to fry, adding the *strutto* and the pork belly. Then she added the *passata* and all the other ingredients, putting it to simmer for two hours. Those who could afford it would add a chunk of beef to the pot.

The aroma that came from the pot was distinctive as the Sunday *sugo*.

Teresa thought that it must come from every house in the valley. It amused her to think that the air in the whole valley was perfumed with it.

Making the *sugo* had distracted the girl for a while, but then Teresa being Teresa could not be sad for too long, it was just not in her nature. It's done, there was nothing to be done about it. What was the point of making herself miserable, and make her mother and father miserable too, adding to their troubles with the worry of what had happened to her. No… she could not do that to them. She decided to be happy and when Teresa had decided something there was no changing her mind.

The *sugo* was ready. She put a large pot full of water on the open fire so that it would be boiling, ready to put the pasta in to cook as soon as everyone was home.

She laid the table. Then she walked to the vegetable garden to gather salad leaves, herbs, tomatoes and cucumbers to make a large salad.

The girl looked about her. It was very strange for her to be in the house alone. She thought of all her brothers and sisters and her eyes filled up with tears. She put down her basket and sat down on a bench that was there for the Nonne to sit and rest while they worked in the allotment.

Soon there would be so many in the house, her

parents, her grandparents, brothers and sisters, yet she felt that she could not talk to anybody. She was ashamed, she felt defiled and unclean, no longer one of them. She could not name what had happened to her.

Teresa dried her eyes. How could Gian Filippo do such a thing? She had liked him and she thought that he liked her. But in her innocence, she had never felt that he liked her in that way. She had enjoyed their talks when he gave her a lift in his car. She had made him laugh. When they met in the house, which was never planned, they smiled at each other.

She knew that, as she got to know him, she no longer saw him as old and unattractive. This thought made her shiver; had she in her simplicity perhaps encouraged him? The young woman thought of the lecture that her mother had given her on the day that she went to the *palazzo* with Don Pasquale: eyes down when she met the sons of the house.

No! No! It was not her fault, she must not blame herself. It was an understood fact that, by custom, by church teaching, by the expectations of parents who sent their daughters to work as maids, they would be safe.

Gian Filippo knew this also. What had come over him to force himself on her, dishonouring her under his own roof. It was the most shameful thing he could do. Was he feeling guilty, was he ashamed of himself? Did he now think that he had to marry her? Did she want to marry him?

She thought of the age difference between them, twenty-two years, but she would not be the first to marry an older man. In fact, there was over twenty years between Donna Beatrice and her husband.

If she married him, would she grow to love him? She thought of her own parents and the love between them. Would she ever have that? There again, she knew of many married couples who hated each other.

Then she thought of the grinding poverty of so many in the valley. All they could think about was working and put food on the table for their many children. To them, love was not important.

Her life would completely change if she married Gian Filippo. She would be Donna Teresa with all that entailed – a life of luxury would open for her.

No! She would not speak of what had happened to her to anyone. She could not bear their look of pity. She would wait and see what happened, he said that he would make it up to her. How?

CHAPTER 15

Maria Comes Back

BOTH THE GRANDMOTHERS, Concetta and Maria, were sitting outside at an old table under the shade of a fig tree. They were busy shelling peas. There was a glut of peas. They both wished that they had the money to buy a refrigerator, nearly everyone had one now, but other families did not have seventeen grandchildren to feed. If they had a fridge, which had a freezer compartment, they could put the peas in there. Concetta had tried the frozen peas – they tasted as if they had just been picked. But the peas they were shelling would not be wasted. Once shelled, the peas would be put in a glass jar with a teaspoon of salt and a teaspoon of sugar, topped up with water and the lid sealed. Then they would put the jars in a black cauldron filled with water, put them on the fire to boil for twenty minutes and leave them in the water to cool. They did this work outside, as they would also do for the *passata*.

Mostly the two grandmothers would talk about their grandchildren – who was doing what, whom they worried about the most and so on.

Maria was saying to Concetta, 'You know, Concetta, I am really worried about Maria, it is not right that she has gone away and we hear nothing from her. Not even a letter now and then just to say that she is well and happy. I am sure that she would want to hear the same from her family. It's a very cruel thing that the nuns do, to allow no contact with the family.'

'But I am not surprised. The church is often like this, very secretive about everything and it may be a sin to say this, but I don't like nuns, especially the old ones as they are often the cruellest of all. I wish we could do something. Matilda has written twice to the Mother Superior, but she has heard nothing back from her. You know, I can't sleep at night for thinking about it.'

'Concetta, I am thinking of hiring a car to take me there. I really want to go. What do you think? Is it a good idea? You can come with me if you want.'

Concetta thought for a moment then said, 'I would very much like to come with you, but how can I? I can hardly move, my rheumatism is so bad, but yes, you go, and I will pay for the car. Now that I have that bit of pension, I can pay. I do hope you will soon get a pension too. I know that you are too young yet, but it's so good to have a wee bit of money of your own so that if you want to give a few coins to a child for an ice cream, you can.'

Later that day, Maria was speaking to Vincenzo and Matilda, telling them of her plans to go to Sora and inquire about Maria and that she wouldn't come back until she had seen her.

'Yes Maria, you do that. Insist, and don't move until you have seen her! I would go with you if I could,' said Concetta.

Vincenzo was distressed. 'Has Maria not got a father? How can two old women, no offence, get in a taxi to go to God only knows where? I have been thinking the same thing for a while and should have done what you say long ago, and now you have made me feel ashamed that I have not done so. Tomorrow morning, I will go and do just as you say: demand to see her and if they refuse, I will stand my ground until they let me.'

Maria was relieved that she did not have to make the journey.

Concetta quickly interjected, 'I was going to pay for the car. I will still pay for the car.'

'No Mamma, save your money, I will go with the autobus, it is not a problem. I have been before.'

The following morning, Vincenzo set off to go to see his daughter. He was soon at Colle Posta sitting on a bench outside the house of his friend Giacomo. From there you could see when the autobus was arriving.

He told Giacomo where he was going.

Giacomo said, 'Yes, children are such a worry. I have not heard from my son Marco for six months. He writes less and less, and I fear he will stop writing altogether. America is such a long way away, it seems that once they go there, they are lost to us forever and it's even worse if they depart for South America, Argentina or Venezuela. These children are dead to their parents. I remember when Marco decided to emigrate. It was just after the war. He said that there was no future for him here. At first, he wanted to go to France, not too far from home. But France at that time, just at the end of the war, was in turmoil like the rest of Europe. He could not find a sponsor. Perhaps the new world had more to offer.

He wrote to your brother-in-law Alfonso to ask him if he could help him find work. He knew that he could not go unless he had a work contract. Alfonso did just that! Found him work at General Motors where he worked himself in New York.

'He lived with Alfonso and his wife for a while, until he found a room of his own to rent in Brooklyn, not far from where Alfonso lived. They have both moved to New Jersey. It is a much better place to live and many other Italians have moved there to get away from the slums of Brooklyn.

'Your son Andrea has gone to *La Scozia*, they come back sometimes. I have heard of parents that were so desperate to hear from their child that they would journey there to find them. Sometimes that is possible, Scotland is not that far, but you can't do that for America.'

Vincenzo nodded his head in agreement looking directly into Giacomo's eyes. Then, changing the subject, 'Do you think you are going to have a good grape harvest this year? The vines are looking healthy.'

'Well, you know what it is like, if you get rain at the right time, if the sun is not too fierce, if there is no attack of pests.' He smiled and slapped his hand on Vincenzo's shoulder. 'You know yourself, when growing things there are so many "ifs" and that is partly why our children leave.'

The bus arrived. Vincenzo climbed on board and sat down, his thoughts went back to what Giacomo had said, that his son had not written to him in six months. Giacomo did not know anything about what was in the letter from America.

The bus took an hour to get to Sora; there he had to change to another bus that went to Casamari, and then make the ten-minute walk to the convent.

It was a long time before someone came to the gate to enquire who was continuously ringing the bell.

'Who are you and what do you want?' he was asked by a well-fed nun.

'I am Vincenzo Valente, I have come to ask permission of the Mother Superior to see my daughter Maria.'

'You do know that there is no contact with the family while she is a novice? And if you know, why are you here?'

She was about to turn away when Vincenzo said to her in a firm tone, 'Sister, I have not come all this way to just turn and go back. Go and tell the Mother Superior that I want to speak to her. Please could you do that?'

Again, he stood for a long time. He decided he would play the waiting game – he was not leaving until he saw Maria.

Eventually, she returned. She said, 'Mother Superior cannot see you now, come back tomorrow, or write to make an appointment.'

'You tell her that I am not leaving here until I have seen my daughter.'

Vincenzo took a walk around the walls and railings of the grounds to see if there was another way in. He could not scale the walls, but he did notice a gate at the back that opened into the vegetable garden. He climbed over the fence. He went to see if the gate was locked. It was not. He went back to the front gate and pulled the bell again and again. If they would not let him in at the front gate, he would go to the back gate; one way or another, he was going to see his girl.

The nun returned to the gate. 'Mother Superior has

said that if you do not go away, she will send for the *carabiniere*.'

By this time Vincenzo was really angry. 'You tell the fucking Mother Superior that I came here to see my daughter, which as her father I have every right to do. I am not a delinquent who wants to abuse anyone, so open this gate and let me in.'

The nun walked away and came back with the key. He was taken to a waiting room, and again he was kept waiting. Eventually, the Mother Superior walked in. She stared at him with a look of disdain and disapproval.

'What can I do for you, my son?'

'Madam,' he said, 'you know why I am here, I just want to see my daughter Maria. I want to see that she is well and happy, after that I will leave. I do not know why you have such cruel rules and inhumane policies. What is the harm of a father seeing his child?'

'My son, we do not make the rules, we just abide by them. I can tell you that Sister Maria is well, she's doing well in her training to take the veil. I know that it is hard for you and other families, but that is just as it is. Again, I can reassure you that she is well, and if you would be so kind as to leave now.'

She turned to go—

'Sister, I am not leaving here until I see my daughter. Make it easy on yourself and bring her here right now. That way, it will be all over and each of us can go on our way. Or I can wait here until tomorrow or even the day after, it's up to you.'

The nun turned to him with a look of panic on her face. She could see that she was not going to win this argument.

'Wait here, I will send her to you,' she said before walking away.

Soon after, Maria appeared at the door, a nun behind her.

'Papà!' she cried as she flew in his arms. 'Oh Papà, I have missed you so much.'

The nun that was there with her interrupted, 'Sister, please control yourself, have you not learned anything about how to behave? Sit down and remember who you are.'

Maria and her father sat down. They eyed the mean-looking nun who stood there, waiting for her to leave, but instead she sat down on a chair beside the door.

The father looked at his daughter. She looked like a shadow of her former self, thin and so pale it was as if she had not seen sunlight for a long time.

They had a stunted conversation. Maria asked about everyone at home. She asked if Mamma had had a boy or a girl, and if he was a good baby.

Vincenzo asked her how she was and whether she was well, did she get enough food…

Vincenzo noticed that she kept looking at the woman who sat at the door. He said to her, 'Is it possible to have some time alone with my daughter?'

'I am sorry, but that is impossible, sisters must be chaperoned at all times.'

'*Va bene*,' he said before turning to Maria. 'I am going to ask you a question and you are going to answer truthfully. Are you happy here?'

The girl started crying.

'Do you want to stay here?'

She sobbed.

'Tell me.'

'No Papà, I am not happy.'

'Do you want to come home?'

'Yes Papà, I want to come home.'

'Run and get your things and we will go home.'

The nun ran to get the Mother Superior. The girl ran to get her things.

Both returned at the same time. The Mother Superior stood in the doorway. She said to the girl, 'You are abandoning God, you will be cursed.'

Vincenzo took his daughter's hand.

'Get out of my way, Sister, and may God forgive you and all of your kind.'

What a surprise it was to the family when Vincenzo arrived home with Maria.

The day after, she wore her own clothes and told her story; she had not liked the nuns, finding them cruel and bitter, and saw they prayed without meaning, especially the old nuns who had long ago lost their faith. She was glad to be home, but now she had lost her dream of going to Africa.

CHAPTER 16

Teresa Again

IT WAS THE FIRST week of August and all the family were back home. Donna Beatrice and her husband were looking tanned and in good health, as were Rosetta and Angelica. All her sons except Gian Filippo were looking equally well. Gian Filippo seemed as if his stay in Rome had not done him any good at all. He should have come with them to get some sea air, said his mother.

Teresa felt nervous to have them all back in the house. Could she cope with the situation as it was now? Surely they would notice the change in her. Could she carry on as normal when she met Gian Filippo? To wait at the table, to clean his room, and so forth. She began to think that she would have to leave, to go home. But to go home to what, to hoe the earth, *a zappare*. She looked at her hands. They were pale and soft, her nails clean, no earth under them. Here she had a bedroom all to herself – it was a small room under the eaves, but she did not share it with anyone. How many did she have to share with at home? Out of curiosity, she counted them on her fingers. Including her grandmother Maria, and now also the twin girls, Lia and Erica, there were ten in one room.

Teresa had already got used to certain luxuries that were unheard of at home. She tossed and turned at night thinking about what to do.

Then one morning she awoke and was about to jump out of bed but sat for a while and thought. Then again she counted on her fingers, but this time she was not counting how many sisters she had. The number in her head was seven. She was seven days late. Her period was late and this was not something that was normal for her.

Yes, she was young and innocent but her mother had had nineteen children so she knew full well what that number meant. No, she wouldn't panic, she would wait another seven days before she would throw herself down 'the cliff of dogs'. This was a steep cliff where people went to throw down dogs that were old or sick or just not wanted. It was quick.

Each day upon awakening she would throw back the bedding and each time there was nothing there. At night when she went to bed, she would kneel by the bed and pray. She would beg, 'Please God, please God, I will do anything. Please Madonna di Canneto, I will walk barefoot all the way up the mountain to see you. I will do this for the next five years.'

Seven days passed. She packed her bag to go home; she knew she did not have to courage to kill herself. She had to face her fate.

But she was angry, very angry. She would not take this lying down.

She thought, what was she to do? What would be best for her, now this child was also to be considered.

Should she tell Gian Filippo and his mother, should she talk to them, or should she get her father and mother to talk to them?

He had raped her, he had abused her. In her bag she still had her ripped, bloodstained underwear.

She thought and thought about what she wanted the outcome to be, and one thought kept going round and round in her head.

She took her bag and walked out of the *palazzo*. At the gate she looked back. She had grown to like the place even though she was just a servant.

Matilda was outside getting the tomatoes ready to make *passata*. She could see Teresa coming home. She had her bag with her.

Oh Lord, she thought, what has happened now?

She was just getting over Maria coming home in a state. She walked about the house like a ghost.

Teresa was soon there. She dropped her bag and ran to her mother, throwing her arms around her. Her child was crying. Her own mother had also come out of the house to see the scene.

'What is it?' Nonna Maria asked. 'What has happened, tell me quick. I can't bear to see you like this.'

They went into the house, all three sat at the table. Teresa asked if Papà was in the house. Her mother said he was in the stable and went to call him.

Vincenzo, Matilda and her mother sat at the table waiting for Teresa to speak.

Teresa told them everything.

For Vincenzo, his wife and Nonna Maria, it felt as if the ceiling and the walls of the room were closing in on them. They were in shock. The father felt pure rage; he wanted to go there and kill the bastard.

Teresa cried, 'What am I going to do? Tell me what is going to happen to me!'

All at once, Nonna Maria stood up, slammed her

hands on the table and said, 'Come with me, we are going there right now. They are not getting away with it again.'

Soon all four were at the front door of the *palazzo*. Maria pulled the bell with such force that Rosetta almost ran to open the door.

They walked right in.

'We want to see your *patrona*, right now, tell her its important.'

Once in the salone, Vincenzo looked for Gian Filippo. He wanted to smash his face in. Fortunately, he was not there, the bastard. Donna Beatrice was there with her husband; the Valentes were not asked to sit down, but they did.

Teresa was the first to speak. '*Signora*, your son Gian Filippo has raped me, he has dishonoured me. I am pregnant with his child. I want to know what you are going to do about it. I have not been to the *carabinieri*, I was keeping quiet about it because I did not want to add the burden of what had happened onto my family. But now there is no hiding it. Please call Gian Filippo, tell him that I want to spit on his face. He has ruined me and I am going to ruin him. Gaeta is where he will be for the next five years, and I don't mean the villa.'

All kinds of possibilities were going through Beatrice's mind. 'Teresa what do you want of me? I know of a doctor in Rome, a good doctor not a quack. He will take care of it.'

'No, I am not killing a child. Then I cannot walk into a church ever again.'

'*Va bene*, you can go to Rome, have the child and then give it up for adoption.'

This was a well-known remedy. A girl would get in trouble, say she was going to Rome as a maid, have the child, give it up and then stay in Rome for good as a maid, or come back if she could not settle there.

Teresa knew this and she was not going to be one of them. 'No, I can't do that either. How would I forgive myself for giving up my child?'

At that moment, Gian Filippo arrived home. Hearing voices in the salon, he headed towards the room.

As he walked in, he saw Teresa and her father, mother and grandmother. His face turned grey, his knees almost gave way.

Matilda had to hold her husband back. Gian Filippo did not have to be told why they were there, or what they were talking about.

Teresa shouted, 'Look what you have done to me!' She passed her hand over her belly.

Beatrice quickly went to her son and pulled him outside, closing the door behind them. Ten minutes passed before they came back in.

Beatrice sat down, tapping her fingers on the arms of her chair, took a deep breath and slowly and calmly said, 'Teresa, this is our position. You will have the child, Gian Filippo will then adopt the child and we will give you a monthly pension for the next twenty years of your life. I think I am being very generous, it will be enough money for a decent dowry for when you get married.'

Teresa responded, 'And who will marry... me?' Teresa looked at her mother, father, and nonna. What was she to do, she put her hands to her face and rocked back and forth.

Nonna Maria stood up to say, 'I think she should keep the child and Gian Filippo should pay an allowance for her and the child for the rest of their lives. After all, he is the father of her child.'

Teresa thought back to the idea that had been going round in her head for days now. It kept coming to the front of her mind.

There was a silence for a while and then Beatrice said, 'Well? What do you say of the offer I have made you?'

Teresa sprang up at this. 'WELL! Will tell you what I want from you, Gian Filippo,' and she went to stand in front of him, 'I want you to marry me. If you want an heir for your *palazzo*, that is the only way you are going to have one.'

His mother gurgled a laugh, she was shocked. 'What, my son marry you?' She looked with disdain on Teresa and her family.

'Yes, marry me or it's Gaeta for him.'

Beatrice laughed again. 'I have money and I have lawyers, my son will not go to prison. So please do not be ridiculous.'

At this point her son stood up. 'Mamma, perhaps it is best for me to do as she says. I will marry her.'

'Sit down Gian Filippo and don't be stupid. I have never heard of anything so absurd, to marry a servant, what will our family and friends think? You will be a laughing stock.'

At this, Nonna Maria walked over to the woman, leaned forward and said to her, 'Beatrice, can I have a word with you in private? Come outside.'

The amusement left Beatrice's face and she went a little pale.

Five minutes passed and they came back in. Then she said to her son, 'If you want to be a laughing stock, so be it. Marry her.'

Teresa looked at Gian Filippo and saw that he was happy at her words. She stood in front of Beatrice, she pulled herself straight and tall and said to her: 'And why should he be laughed at? Look at me, I am beautiful, young, healthy and I carry his child, he will be envied.'

They were soon on their way home. When they reached the gravel drive, Matilda asked her mother, 'Mamma, what did you say to her in private, outside?'

It was Maria's turn to laugh now. 'That is between Beatrice and I, we go a long way back her and me.'

Teresa stopped and said, 'Wait here, I am going back inside.'

When she returned, a car appeared from around the corner and stopped. Gian Filippo was driving. Teresa got in the front seat and said to her folks to get in too. They were not going to walk home… why should they, now that she was to be the lady of the house?

***

Teresa was on the edge of the bed. Anyone else would fall out, but her body was used to it and knew when it was in danger. Stefania had cuddled into her back. Teresa lay there with her eyes closed, but she was not asleep.

She was in the villa. She was on the balcony, sitting

on a wicker chair with cushions, the bougainvilleas were climbing over the railing and she could see the sea. She rang the bell for iced tea.

She was walking on the palm-lined promenade, on her feet were espadrille sandals and she wore a flowing, flowery dress with a slim belt and shoulder straps. Her skin was golden brown and luminous, on her head a large straw hat.

She was on the beach sitting on a stripped deck chair under an umbrella, at her side a child played in the sand.

In none of these fantasies she could see Gian Filippo, but she was not worried. She would grow to love him, and once she had made her mind up, there was no changing it.

CHAPTER 17

Festa Time

IN THE VALLEY surrounded by mountains, there were about ten towns, some small like Villa Latina with around one thousand inhabitants, and others like Picinisco and Atina which had three times as many. Each town had many villages and hamlets. August was the time when most, but not all, of the towns celebrated the *festa* for their patron saint. August was also the month when many young people who had left to work far from home – to work for a better life for themself and their children, to get away from poverty, to study or for other reasons of their own – would come home to their mothers' open arms.

Those who worked up North, in Milan, Turin, Brescia, usually came back for *Ferragosto*, the fifteenth of the month. Factories would close for two weeks. These young people would come back well-dressed, speaking the correct Italian language and looking down their noses at *zappare*. These people did not feel homesick. After all, they were still in *Italia*.

The young men and women who had gone further afield, to Belgium, Germany, etc, also came back in August so that they would not miss the *festa* of their hometown. They were the ones who missed *Italia*, the people, the food, their family and friends. They were in a strange land; a different language and customs, often mistreated and told to go back to where they came from. But the money was good, so they stayed.

Then there were the other sons and daughters who had gone to *La Gran Bretagna*. They could not believe their luck. Yes, they had to work hard to finish their four-year contract and they needed that blessed five pounds to get into the country. Often that same five pounds went back and forwards between brothers and cousins. But the advantages were so many.

Healthcare was free and you could send your children to a good school. Occasionally, they were told that they were an Italian bastard and to go back to where they came from. Some people really did not like them because of the war and Mussolini. But on the whole people were kind and lent a hand.

These people who left with a cardboard suitcase came back with a small car, nice white teeth – dentists were free – and with a wife and child in tow, or came back to choose a wife.

They would bring gifts to give to their relatives, tea and chocolate, drip-dry shirts that needed no ironing, and Crimplene dresses and skirts that their mothers would not manage to wear out in their lifetimes.

August was festive in the valley. Then the end of the month would come, the visitors would leave and the towns and villages would go back to sleep.

The Valente family were getting ready to go to Canneto. Not all of them were going – Nonno Andrea would see to the animals and Nonna Concetta could not go anywhere with her bad knees. Matilda was not fully recovered after having Lorenzo and she did not want to leave him; she was still bringing him back and forth to Adelina to be fed. Some of the boys were not interested in going to Canneto with the family and would spend the holidays in their own way. This also applied to Teresa now that she was engaged to Gian Filippo – her life was going in a different direction.

Vincenzo and Nonna Maria set off with a group of the children. The feast of *La Madonna di Canneto* was held in a deep valley in the mountains.

They brought their food with them, each carrying something. They would walk there to join many other pilgrims on the road. First, they would walk all the way up to Picinisco, then to Fontitune where they would stop for a drink at Anna's house, then on to the path that went all the way to Canneto and finally to the majestic cathedral for mass. After the celebration of the Holy Mass was over, the boys and girls would leave to wander around the stalls that were selling religious memorabilia, trinkets and the usual roasted peanuts and toys. Then they would make their way to the appointed place, where they would all meet.

Nonna Maria and Concettina followed the children, looking here and there as they made their way to the grassy area beside the river. There they would meet many neighbours and family. They went by the river to dip their feet into the cool water. In the shallows, children were looking for shiny stars. It was said that when Our Lady came here in ancient times, there was no water. She banged the rock with her hand and made the water gush out of the rock as it did now. The diamond ring she was wearing shattered into a thousand pieces and that was what the children were trying to catch.

Maria and Concettina went back to sit beside their basket of food and wait for everyone to come so that they could eat. They didn't mind waiting as they were enjoying themselves, sitting and chatting to people they knew well. Not far from them, over the little wooden bridge, was another gathering having a good time, with the *organetto* already playing.

Vincenzo stayed in the church. He wanted some time on his own in the peace of the empty sanctuary before it would fill again with pilgrims for the next mass. He wanted to give thanks for the safe outcome of Matilda's delivery of his son Lorenzo. He sat and looked around him, this house of God with its many saints in century-old garments, dusty and falling apart with age, holding miniatures of the instrument by which they had died to become a martyr and flowers and candles at their feet.

Our Lady of Canneto was on the altar in prime place – after all, this was her *festa*. She was surrounded by candles of all sizes and flowers, both extravagant bouquets and simple pots with daisies.

As he sat there, feeling the peace, he could hear from outside that a *compania* of pilgrims had arrived. The traditional *Zampognare*, a band of men dressed in the folk costumes of the area, with *ciocia*, homemade sandals.

The ancient, carved wooden door was opened, and the pilgrims streamed in. First came the music, followed by the banners carried high stating the town they were from, then the devotees followed. On their necks they wore similar scarves to show that they were all from the same town. Some Christians came on bare feet and some carried candles and flowers.

They had come from Aquino, a town past Cassino, about sixty miles away. It had taken them two days to walk here. The musician played ancient instruments: *la zampogne*, a kind of bagpipe, a flute and the most ancient of them all, a *biffer*. The music, along with the singing and its heart-rending soulful pitch, filled the church. They sang 'Ave Maria' and the sound went somewhere deep inside that made you choke with emotion.

Vincenzo was feeling this.

Once everyone was inside, the priest who had come with his congregation stood on the altar and raised his voice to call on Our Lady, '*EVVIVA MARIA!*'

The pilgrims then also called out in a high voice, '*EVVIVA MARIA!*'

The priest implored, 'Hail Mary, we are here again to see you, let your blessing be on us.'

Vincenzo walked to a side door that led down to the crypt. There was a long room, the walls covered with all kinds of objects to represent different parts of believers' bodies that had been cured of life-threatening diseases or those whose prayers for a miracle after an accident had been answered.

At the end of the room there was an office with a counter. A monk asked him what he could do for him. He had a pen and notebook in front of him.

Vincenzo told him that he wanted a mass dedicated to the souls of his grandparents, and also Matilda's grandparents and her father, Pietro. He listed all their names, which the monk wrote down.

'I also want to make an offering for Grace received,' Vincenzo said.

'What Grace was that my son?'

'The safe delivery of my son Lorenzo.'

The Holy man wrote it down. Vincenzo gave him some money and left.

Once outside of the church, he stood for a while in the bright sunlight. He took it all in, the mountain on all sides, rich in trees. He could just see the peak of *la Meta*.

Then he noticed a group of people all looking at a particular part of the mountain. Of course, he thought, they are looking for the boy. He looked himself and saw that the boy was still there. A man came up to him and asked what everyone was looking at. He showed him.

'Look,' he said, 'at that piece of the mountain. At a certain point there is the head of a boy, if you keep looking you will see him.'

The man looked and looked. 'All I see is the mountain,' and he was about to give up. Vincenzo left him to go on his way. Then he heard him, 'Yes, yes, I can see him now!' Vincenzo looked back to smile at him. That was just how it always was. You could see nothing and then all at once he was there. The head of a perfect boy. Vincenzo would check every year to see if he had aged, or if the vegetation and rocks that made him had also made him disappear.

He joined the rest for his meal – he was quite hungry. On the way there he bought a little trinket for Matilda, a little cameo brooch with the *Madonna di Canneto*.

Soon after the *festa di Canneto*, followed the *festa di Santa Maria*. This was the biggest celebration the town of Picinisco would host. The population doubled on that day. It was a *festa* not to be missed. People came from far and wide to be there.

The Valente family would also celebrate as best as they could. Certainly, there was much they could not afford: new outfits for all the children were out of the question and buying meat for all of them was also out of their league. They did go to Picinisco in the morning to go to the mass. Then back home for their own celebration. The tables in the kitchen were taken out and placed under the fig tree. The girls set it for all of them, decorated it with flowers and branches, and managed to find seating for all. Music was playing on the radio that Andrea had sent from Scotland. It was old and reconditioned, but it worked.

Matilda and the grandmothers had been busy getting ready for the feast, all hands on board.

Nonno Andrea was beside the oven, controlling the operation. When the bread and biscuits were ready, he would take them out, then in would go all the rest.

At last, all was ready. They sat down, and after much deliberation everyone was settled.

The menu for the *festa di Santa Maria* included a starter of *prosciutto* parma ham with figs, then the pasta dish was lasagna, followed by four roast chickens with delicious stuffing, roasted vegetables, stuffed peppers, baked potatoes and salad. There was also cake, biscuits dipped in white wine and of course no *pranzo* would be a feast without *cocomero*, watermelon.

It was all their own produce apart from the minced beef for lasagna and the watermelon.

Vincenzo and Matilda sat and relaxed. They looked at their children, happy and laughing, singing and dancing to the music on the radio. Who needs friends when you had seventeen brothers and sisters to party with? The three older people that lived in the house wondered if they would ever have peace and quiet again, with the radio blaring. They went inside for a nap. Later, those who wanted to would go to Picinisco for the candlelit procession and fireworks.

CHAPTER 18

Wedding Plans

VINCENZO WAS SITTING with his wife beside him. They were talking about the wedding. Pietro was getting married on the ninth of September, only two weeks away.

Matilda said, 'It is true what the older people say: small children, small problems; big children, big problems. Up to now we have coped, we have managed to feed them and brought them up well. But with this wedding, the first of many, I have this feeling of panic, that I can't cope. There is so much to do, and with money that we do not have. What are we to do?'

Vincenzo responded, 'Yes, you are right, and as you say, it is the first of many. There is one good thing, Pietro has been working at the soap factory for three months so that bit of money is a Godsend.'

'I have been looking through the children's clothes and passing the Sunday best down to the next child. Also, my mother and yours are making and remaking the younger children's clothes, but the older girls want new dresses and you cannot blame them – they want to look their best. I will take the girls to the market now that you can buy clothes readymade. They can choose something there; it's so much cheaper than buying material to take to the seamstress. I will get something there for me too. The tailor is charging quite a bit for your suit, but he is using good material so I don't mind because you can use that suit again and again… if you don't put on a belly!'

The clothes were put aside and Vincenzo moved on to talk about the catering. 'We have already spoken to Ciccio, he and his family will do the catering. They will bring the *tendone*, marquees, and all the tables, chairs, cutlery, napkins, glasses, tablecloths, the lot, and outdoor cooking equipment. We will provide the food and they will cook it. So don't worry about that. They have done it many times before, they know what they are doing. I know that it will cost money, but it is money well spent. Of course, we will pay for our guests and Anna's father will pay for the relatives that he invites... and for the first time I am thinking I am lucky to be an only child! And you too, your only brother is in America... but we have made up for not having relatives, we have children!' He roared with laughter.

Matilda's face relaxed, 'We have all the foodstuff, we will start to prepare next week. With Pietro's money, we have already bought Anna's wedding dress, and the gold ring and necklace. So that is already paid for. Pietro has also paid the first three months' rent for the house. Franco is fixing it for them, new windows and doors.

'Next week they are bringing down her dowry, linen and furniture. Pietro's suit is also being made. We will have to pay the tailor in instalments for that because we have so many other expenses,' she continued.

'There is no need for us to hire a musician. Franco said he has many relatives who can play the *organetto*,' Vincenzo added.

'Maybe *tutto va bene*, all will be well,' she mused. 'But I am so nervous, maybe because it is our first wedding. When we get to wedding number seventeen, it will all come easy to us and we will not worry at all. At least we do not have to worry about Teresa, because she married quietly.'

She and Gian Filippo travelled to Rome and married with only his brothers and Concettina and Maria as witnesses. Gian Filippo's parents felt too ashamed to take part in their son's folly. Vincenzo and Matilda were not invited. The couple were away on their honeymoon to Venezia.

'It will be interesting to see if they come to Pietro's wedding, or whether Gian Filippo would, like his mother, feel it was beneath him to attend. Then again, he seemed besotted by his young bride, maybe he would come just to make her happy.'

Just then, Francesco came to sit by them for a minute. He had decided to follow his brother to Scotland. He would have gone before now if he had not promised Pietro that he would be there for his wedding.

He already had his train ticket to leave on the fourteenth of September. Vincenzo thanked God that Andrea had sent him the five pounds and his ticket, because there was no way that he could have helped him with it. He said to his son, 'You're going away, Andrea has already gone, Teresa has married, Pietro is soon to be married, there will be no one left at home.' All three smiled, but no one laughed, because in a way it was sad that the family was breaking up.

***

The wedding day came. They were ready, or as ready as they could ever be. Pietro, his father and mother left first with Mediucci, because they were going to Fontitune. The grandparents stayed at home to look after the little one and mind the house as there were so many people there getting the wedding feast ready. The rest of the family walked to Picinisco to meet the bride and groom, then followed them with the rest of the company to the church for the ceremony.

All the house was ready; the tables were set, food cooking, radio on, courtyard swept, chickens in their coop and animals tended to.

The bride and groom walked down the track with everyone else following behind, *organetto* playing. Time for fun, food and drink.

'*Salute e figli maschi!*' (May your first child be male!)

When the meal was finished, the dancing began in earnest. No one could beat the people from up-by when it came to having a good time. Franco and his family were soon up dancing *la ballarela*, dancing with either a male or female partner, *la polca* or *valzer*.

The young men would get all the girls up to dance. Friends and neighbours came to watch, young men and women came from all over to dance. At a wedding, after the meal was over, anyone could come to dance, you did not need an invitation.

Such a good time was had. The mountain folk knew how to enjoy a *festa*.

CHAPTER 19

Francesco

SEPTEMBER WAS THE MONTH of 'mists and mellow fruitfulness'. The hay season was over and the *passata* made. The rest of the late tomatoes on the vine would be cut in half and dried in the sun. The green bunches would be hung in the hay loft, where they would ripen slowly, sometimes as late as Christmas.

The surplus vegetables would be bottled. Red peppers were roasted and put in jars with garlic and *olio* and put in a *bagnomaria*, a bain-marie, for a short while. This was food for the winter months. Fruit and nuts were also stored, dried or jarred. Nothing was wasted; their depleted *despensa* had to be restocked.

The young children had returned to school and just that morning Matilda had kissed goodbye to another one of her children.

Don Pasquale had come to the house with a hired car. He was going to Sora. He had to go to a meeting with the diocese that was responsible for all the parishes in the valley and since he was going, he said that he would take Osvaldo with him.

Osvaldo had been accepted at the school in Sora. He had passed his exam with top marks. Don Pasquale was really pleased with him, proud that he had not let him down. His parents were also proud of him, not missing any opportunity to tell people that he got a bursary to go to the elite college.

Matilda was glad for him. This time, she and her husband had asked many questions to reassure themselves that he would be alright. They did not want a repeat of what had happened to Maria.

Yes, they could write to him and he could write to them. They could visit anytime to put their mind at rest that he was doing well. He would come home for the holidays. They were reassured and when he left that morning it had been a cheerful goodbye.

Francesco would also leave the following morning. That would be a different goodbye. Two sons away into the unknown, so far away. Andrea seemed happy and his letters were frequent. In his last letter, he had told his mother that he would telephone her, which was something completely new to her. He had said that next time he sent a letter, he would tell her exactly what to do. Maybe when Francesco arrived she could speak to them both. It will be so good to hear his voice, my darling boy.

Francesco had his bag packed. In the suitcase, Matilda had put in the last of the sausages and a piece of her best *prosciutto*, dried figs and a round of the best pecorino cheese that Anna had given her, made with the milk from the high summer pasture. A taste of home for him.

That night she would make Francesco his favourite, *tagliolini* with porcini mushrooms that she had found behind the hayloft. She would make the meal early because she knew that he would be dying to go to say goodbye to his girl, Catarina. She had heard that she was distraught because he was going away.

Francesco ate the *tagliolini* with porcini mushrooms and he enjoyed every mouthful, the last meal with his family. He was sad to go; just the thought of it made his eyes fill up. Was this really… what he wanted? Yes, he thought to himself, he had to go and make a success of his life. He wanted to marry Catarina, but if he stayed here how could he? No job, no house, no money. Catarina had pleaded with him not to go. They could get married, he could work for her father. She had implored her father to tell him that there was a job for him, but he was too proud to accept the offer. He had to try his luck abroad. When he came back to marry her, at least he would have earned some money.

He was at her door. Should he go up to say goodbye? Yes, he would. He pushed the door and went upstairs. He called, 'Hello, it's just me.'

'Come in,' she said.

They were all there, her parents and her sisters. He said to her father, '*Va bene* if we go for a *passeggiata*?'

He nodded his head in agreement, 'You are going away tomorrow, then?'

'Yes, early, so I want to say goodbye now.'

Catarina's father held out his hand. 'Have a good journey and good luck. Don't forget us, and if things are not to your liking, there is a place for you here.'

He then bid goodbye to Zia Rosina and gave the girls a kiss and a hug. All of them wished him well.

He and Catarina walked down the stairs. At the bottom he embraced her, kissed her. It seemed as if he could never get enough of her.

They walked along the street, both quiet. They had

said all there was to say. She had cried, pleaded, begged him not to go. But she had failed. He had not changed his mind. His only promise was that he would come back to marry her.

They walked and walked, holding hands. She did not care who would see them. The young couple walked past the point at which they would normally turn back. They turned left onto a road that made a wide circle, passing the church and *piazza*. They would end up where they had started.

Every now and again, he would pull her to him to kiss her, always looking over his shoulder to see if they were alone.

They came to an old building used for storing hay and farm implements. In a dark corner, they let their passion loose. He took her hand and pulled her inside the hayloft, pushing the door shut with his foot.

The young man and woman strolled home, wishing the clocks would stop. At the bottom of the stairs going up to the house, they shared a last passionate kiss and a promise of undying love. He held her close, inhaling her scent, feeling the softness of her body, closing his eyes so that the feeling would distil in his mind.

CHAPTER 20

Giovanni

FRANCESCO HAD LEFT for Scotland. Giovanni wondered exactly where this country was. He tried to recall if it had been mentioned in geography lessons. He remembered that the country was part of *La Gran Bretagna* and they spoke English, but he could not place Scotland on the map. If he had an atlas, he could look it up. There was a battered old atlas in the house they had all used. One of the children must have it.

Giovanni's education had come to an end. This year he would not be returning to school. He had passed his exams for *la quinta elementare*. He had finished primary school and that was enough for him. In fact, the only one of his siblings to carry on after that had been Osvaldo. He remembered what a sacrifice it had been for his parents to find the money for his books. He supposed that it had been worthwhile – he was sure that Osvaldo would make something of himself.

Giovanni didn't believe that life was for him, and he was also never going to Scotland. He would stay here to help his folks, to work the land. They really needed him now. All at once, in a few short months, he had become his father's right-hand man. He was the eldest son now that Andrea and Francesco, Osvaldo and Pietro were all away. He knew Pietro was not far, only along the road, but all the same, he was no longer at home. He had his own house now that he was married.

Just the other day, Pietro was at home speaking to his father. Giovanni was there too. Now that he was a man, he sat with the men. Giovanni smiled at this new family set-up.

Pietro was talking about his father-in-law. He had given Anna some money as a wedding gift. In fact, they had received the cash on their wedding night, when they had eventually managed to get away from the folks that were partying, serenading them and throwing gravel at their window. On the bed there was a wad of money. Anna said that it was from her father. Apparently, it is the custom of the shepherds of Fontitune to do this. Of course, Franco and Benedetta could afford to do it; they only had three daughters.

'I was thinking,' he said, 'once I have saved a bit of money from my wage, plus what Anna can put towards it, we will have enough to put down a deposit for a small tractor, or maybe a reconditioned one. Then I can plough your field, Papà. You won't have to break your back, and you will have more time to earn some money because now you need it. Things are changing, as you have seen yourself.

'And as I was saying, a tractor does not just plough, you can get all different attachments that do everything you need to work the land. I can use it at the end of the week, and during the week after I have finished at the factory. I will earn extra cash by ploughing other people's fields, and as soon as we have enough money saved, you could give us a little bit of land so we can start to build our own house.'

Yes, thought Giovanni, that is the way to go. That is

what he wanted to do too, to get on well in *Italia*. He didn't want to leave his family.

He had time to think, after all; herding a few sheep and goats left you plenty of time to think and to look around you, to be aware of what people were doing. He could see people working on the land. Soon it would be time for *la vendemmia*, the grape harvest. After that, it would be olives that had to be picked. All the family would take part. Of course, they only had a few trees, but they would work for other farmers that had plenty of land. Olive trees were often planted on the steep hillside where it would be impossible to grow anything else. The family would get paid in *olio* to add to their storeroom.

He was herding his small flock of animals to Mallarino. The river at this time of the year did not have much water, and the sheep, especially the goats, liked to forage along the bank. He was letting the animals grab a mouthful here and there along the edge of the road until he could let them free to help themselves along the dry part of the riverbed.

Giovanni had a packed lunch with him in a cloth bag with a strap, which he had over his shoulder. By the end of the day, he always wanted to have something in the bag to take home to his mother. He remembered, when he was small, the look of pleasure on his mother's face when he did this. In season, his eyes were always looking; doing so was second nature to him. At this time of the year, it would be mushrooms or fruit.

The boy had just got to a bridge. At its side there was a steep path that led down to the river. He headed the flock down there and left them to go their own way, a mouthful here and another there, and by the end of the day they would have a full belly.

They would slowly make their way up the river and, by the afternoon, he knew that the animals would go faster and faster as they got closer to a certain tree that they knew. It was an oak tree and at this time of the year the ground under it would be littered with acorns, which the animals loved.

He followed slowly after them, checking bushes to see if there was anything there. He checked the pools to see if he could see a trout, he scanned the gravel bed of the river to see if he could see anything that had been brought down when the water was in full flow. As he was doing that, he noticed a glint of sunlight in the distance reflecting on something. He went to investigate. As he got closer to it, he saw that it was a large piece of metal. His heart missed a beat at the thought of what he could do with it. As he went to take a closer look, he saw the object was buried in the gravel. He was sure that it was a large piece of shrapnel. He went towards the object to give it a nudge with his foot and dislodge it from the gravel.

BOOM!

The air all around made the trees sway as if there was a fierce wind.

Vincenzo was working in the vegetable garden. He was hoeing a row of cabbages, checking them for slugs and white butterfly eggs. After he had done that, he sprinkled wood ash all over them and around the roots. Cabbage was a winter crop that he could not do without and after the first frost it was extra tasty. Cooked with cannellini beans and pig skin sausage, dished on to stale bread, left a while to soak in all the juices, and on top a little drizzle of olive oil. It was a winter feast.

He stopped to straighten his back, took a hanky out of his back pocket and wiped his face and the back of his neck. He listened to the silence in the air; it was the sort of quiet that you could only find in the countryside. He could hear the birds chirping. He smiled – he could hear the beat of the butterflies' wing, the distant bleating of lambs in the pens calling for their mother, the munching of his cows chewing the cud and his horse on its forward motion as it cropped the grass. He replaced the red rag in his pocket and went back to the hoeing and thinking. Land work left you with plenty time to think.

BOOM!

He straightened up as he felt a breeze passing by. He looked around him. What was that? He looked towards his house. He could see Giovanni walking down the track coming home. He listened for the sound to come again. There was complete silence – the birds had stopped singing, the horse and the cow raised their heads to listen…

A farmer who lived beside the river, but far enough that his house was safe if there was a springtime flood as the snow melted, also heard the boom. It came from Mallarino.

The farmer walked over to see what that bang was all about. He knew what it sounded like because it was not that long ago that he had heard it many times as he and his family sheltered in the safety of the cellar of his house.

He scrambled down the steep side of the river. He crossed the water on stepping stones that were there for that purpose. In the distance he could see a red patch. What could that be? As he got closer, he let out a cry of sheer horror. He knew the boy. His face was still recognisable. The rest of him was a mangled mess.

'*Madonna mia, Madonna mia, o Dio mio*,' he cried. He looked at the boy; he was young and innocent. He took his jacket off to cover the boy's face and he ran to tell his folks.

Vincenzo could see Gerardo making his way across the field. He was almost running. He started to walk towards him – something had happened. They were face-to-face. Gerardo was red-faced, sweaty and out of breath. They looked at each other, Gerardo terrified to tell, Vincenzo terrified to hear.

'I am sorry, my friend, but something terrible has happened to your son Giovanni,' he said before explaining the condition he had found him in.

'No, that can't be possible. I just saw my son Giovanni coming home!' He called for his son, 'Giovanni! Giovanni! Giovanni!'

Matilda came out of the house wiping her hands on her apron. 'Giovanni is not here he has taken the sheep to graze in Mallarino.'

'No, that is not possible, I just saw him coming home!'

'Giovanni, Giovanni!' he called as his knees gave way under him.

CHAPTER 21

They Come to a Decision

THEY HAD NOT let her see her son. The *carabinieri* had made sure of it. She had screamed and screamed that she wanted to see him. Eventually Vincenzo had to tell her, 'It is best that you do not see him, I have seen him and wished to God I had not!'

The image would haunt him for the rest of his life. The sadness in the house was almost palpable, thick in the air. From the grandparents to the young ones, everyone missed him.

Two-year-old Bruno kept asking for him, saying, 'I want to play with Gianni, Mamma where is Gianni?'

Matilda went into a kind of dream world. All at once she did not just want Giovanni but also Andrea and Francesco. All three melted into one in her hazy dreams.

She would disappear without saying anything. Concettina would look for her, asking people as she searched if anyone had seen her. Yes, they had seen her walking towards Picinisco. At last, Concettina had found her in the cemetery, sitting beside her son's grave. Now when she disappeared, they knew where she would be.

Six weeks had passed when, one afternoon, Matilda walked out of the house with a piece of paper in her hand. She walked along a lane to find her husband who was fixing a fence. She sat on a tree trunk as Vincenzo went to stand beside her. No more bad news, please God, he thought.

'Is that a letter from one of the boys?'

'No, it is the letter from my brother,' she said before reading the letter to him again.

'What are you thinking about then?'

'I am thinking about our life and the lives of our children. We work and work and with their help we manage, but what is there for them here, what is there for their future? We at least have the land that your father left you, you are an only child.

'I am beginning to hate this country that has nothing to offer our children, that they have to leave. The best of this land, their blood the purest and sweetest of this place.

'If only there was some help for the people that tilled the land in bad years so that we could make it to the next. Then their only solution would not be to abandon the land and leave. If only there was more work like the soap factory, so that people could top up what they got from the land. Then they would have something put aside for when there was a drought, flood, plague or disease. These children that leave don't do so because they want to leave their parents behind to grow old without the comfort of their grandchildren. They leave because they want a future for their children. When you and I were young, if we had enough food, we were happy. But now they want so much more. There is so much to want out there, you just need money.'

Vincenzo was listening to his wife. He had never heard her speak in this way, from somewhere deep within. The loss of Giovanni had changed her. She would never be the same. He hoped that with time she would find peace and resume her life for the sake of the other children who needed her.

He knew that he was in a bad way himself. He could not get out of his mind the image of Giovanni when he had run to Mallarino. At night he would dream of Giovanni walking home. But he never made it. He would never get over it, but he must be strong. He could not afford to break down.

He asked her, 'What should we do about what that letter says, are you thinking what I am thinking?'

'I think that you should write to him. Tell him that he has to take the twins, Antonio and Giuseppe, so that they have each other and will not get homesick, and that he has to adopt them legally, so that his property goes to them.'

Vincenzo nodded his head, 'Yes, it will be good for them. They will grow up there, go to school, learn the language. They will grow up to love their uncle as their father.' He choked back a sob at this and continued in a broken voice. 'When they grow up, they will not have to leave, to go all on their own to another country. You know... that it will be hard for us after what has just happened, will you be alright?'

'It is *because* of what happened to my son. If Giovanni was not on the lookout for bits of metal that he could sell to the scrap merchant to get a few coins, if we could have given him a few coins, he would still be alive.

'It will be hard for us, but it is best for them. We will ask them, see what they think, give them time to think about it. I know that they are only ten years old, but they are smart.'

Vincenzo responded, 'I have been thinking about the other thing in the letter that Alfonso sent us from America. Your brother said that Giacomo's son Marco has asked him if we would allow him to marry one of the girls.'

Matilda looked up to listen.

'I have been thinking about Maria. Since she has come back, she is neither here nor there, she is like a soul that has lost its way. Would a complete change do her good, to start a new life, get married and have children? These things could breathe new life into her. Should we give her a choice, either to do that, or go with the boys to stay with her uncle? Maybe there she will have many more opportunities, even another convent if that is what she wants. They all can't be as bad as the one in Sora. I think that was why they took her without a dowry, no one wants to go there. It must have a bad reputation, shame we didn't know that before.'

With bitterness and sadness, they agreed to sleep on it, see how they felt tomorrow.

The following day, they spoke to their parents to see what their thoughts were. They were wiser and had more experience of life. Nonno Andrea and his wife both nodded in agreement, but the grandfather warned them to be prepared that one day the boys would ask why them…

Nonna Maria was happy about the plan. She was happy for her son who was childless. She said in response to Andrea, 'That may be the case, but once they grow up and see all the opportunities they have there, they will thank you for making the sacrifice. And you know, Matilda, one day they will come back to see us. I am sure that my son will want to see me before I die. Maybe we could go to visit them. You can go on a plane now and be there in twenty-four hours. America is not the end of the earth anymore. Think of it in that way my dear.'

Antonio and Giuseppe were shocked when their mamma and papà told them what they had in mind.

They had to explain to them that it was not because they loved them less than their brothers and sisters. It was because they were twins, so they had each other and would never be alone. The boys looked like two peas in a pod. They could talk to each other without speaking. But it was up to them, it was fine if they didn't want to go.

They reassured the boys about going to America. Zio would be waiting for them. They explained as simply as possible the reasons why they should go. They spent as much time as they could with them, always making sure to remind them that if they did not want to go, no one was going to insist.

When Vincenzo and Matilda spoke to Maria, it was much easier. She understood right away what her choice was, and her answer was also easy. Without a second thought, she decided that she would marry Marco, even if she did not love him. Marco also wanted to marry her, without love. That was fine, it suited them both. They would form a family and get on. If love should grow between them, that would be an added bonus. She knew Marco, he was much older than her, but at least he was from these parts and they had people in common. She had heard of girls going to America to marry strangers, a husband they did not know, arranged by a marriage broker.

'Yes,' she said to her mamma and papà. 'I will do as you suggest. I will pray to God to make a success of my life. It's for the best that I go. I will be sad to leave my family, but I will look forward to the future.'

When Antonio and Giuseppe heard that Maria was going too, they agreed to go now that they were all going together.

Letters were sent back and forth to America. It took time, which turned out to be a good thing as it gave them a chance to prepare and come to terms with the departure. There were also many things to see to; clothes to buy, shoes, coats. Money came from overseas, and it was done.

The arrangement for legal papers was more difficult. A passport had to be applied for as well as a document that provided consent for the boys to travel, which their parents had to sign in front of a judge.

Then the 'wedding'. It was something that Maria had insisted on. She would not go without a contract, a marriage certificate. Therefore, a marriage was arranged. Maria and Giacomo had to go to the *Palazzo Communale* with witnesses, the father standing in proxy for his son Marco. Maria would get a marriage certificate, and travel as a married woman.

It was all done. Giacomo and Vincenzo hired

Mediucci to take the young woman and the boys to Naples, where they would board a ship to take them to the land of milk and honey, where the streets were paved with gold. There was not much talk on their return journey. Vincenzo felt as if a horse had kicked him in the stomach.

CHAPTER 22

Stefania

STEFANIA WAS A fresh-faced girl with dark hair and big curls. She had blue eyes, the only one in the family to do so.

Nonna Concetta would say, 'She looks just like me! Oh yes, I was a beauty in my time, eyes as blue as the sky on a summer day. Andrea fell for my eyes at first sight, he did. He always said so.'

Stefania was a middle child. There were the 'big ones' and the 'little ones', but being in the middle meant she was nearly always overlooked. There was a six-year gap between her and Concettina, and a five-year gap between her and her nine-year-old little sister Fiorinda. Now there was no one in between. She missed them! It felt really strange for the girl. Was she lonely? Was it possible that in this family one could feel lonely? Yes, it was. She missed Giovanni the most. He had been the next youngest and she had held his hand to make sure he did not fall while he explored his world.

Two years had passed since she had finished school. She had passed her *quinta elementare* with flying colours, but no one had noticed, no one congratulated her. Everyone was too interested in what Osvaldo was doing. He was doing brilliantly, but he was not the only one with brains. She felt that if she were also given an opportunity, she would do well too. That was just as it was, boys first. Girls were expected just to marry and have children. While she wanted to do that, she could also do something with her mind.

Her mother and father had suggested that she should apply as an apprentice for the seamstress in Picinisco, or even the tailor if she wanted to do something more challenging. He usually only took boys, but might make an exception for her. An apprenticeship with the seamstress was three long years, and even longer with the tailor. Her pay would be a pittance.

No, she did not want to do that, it sounded so dull. What she really wanted to do was become an engineer. Something that meant you had to use your brain, not your hands. To solve problems, to discover how things worked and how to make them work. The idea had come to her through her teacher – he told her that she had the brains for it.

She stopped herself. It was a pie in the sky, a silly dream. Such a dream was not for the likes of her. She would not mind becoming a teacher, or even working in an office in the *comune*, learning to use a typewriter. But they would not even consider her with just her elementary certificate. If only she could go back to school to study for the *superiore* – she could do it easily and use Osvaldo's books so her parents would not have to go to any extra expense.

She had said this to her mother, but she had discouraged her. What was the point? She already knew enough, she did not need more schooling and in two or three years she would be married and what good would it do? She needed her to help in the house now that she was a 'big one', with six little brothers and sisters. Stefania put her thoughts aside, but she was not happy. Was her only option to become a dressmaker? She would rather die. The boredom of making the same clothes: same women, same style, same material. She would go mad. No, she had to think of something else.

Stefania loved to read; she would read anything. She had read all of Osvaldo's books, her nonna's prayer book, all the labels on any medicines which were in the house. She wished there was a bible in the house she could read. Sometimes Catarina brought her magazines, which she devoured, but she would soon finish them and had to resort to reading them again and again.

When she could get away and she was really bored, as she often was, she would go to visit her sister Teresa.

She had been told to came as often as she liked, but Stefania only went to visit her sister when she knew that Gian Filippo was not at home. She felt so uncomfortable when he was there. She did not like the way he was with her sister, always touching her, kissing her caressing her belly, almost as if she was his property. She knew that something bad had happened to Teresa while she worked there as a maid.

Many times, she had seen her sister in tears, which was not like Teresa. Stefania had asked her sister what was wrong, but she had just walked away from her. At other times, she saw her mother and Nonna talking quietly and as soon as she approached them, they would stop talking and tell her to go outside.

For a week or two, the calm everyday atmosphere in the house had changed. There was a secret. What was there to hide? It was something that she and all her younger sisters and brothers were not allowed to know. But Concettina, her mother and father, and the grandparents knew.

Stefania could see them whispering to each other, with a worried look on their faces.

Then, all at once, Teresa said she was going to marry Gian Filippo. Stefania could not believe it, but it was a true. And after a couple of weeks, she did. Teresa went to Rome to get married and within two months she was already pregnant. Gian Filippo and his parents were delighted about the baby that was soon to be born.

When she did go to visit, she would go through the back door to the kitchen. Rosetta would go to tell Teresa that she was there. This time, Rosetta came back and said to her that the lady of the house wanted her to join her in the *piccolo salone*. Rosetta led the way, Stefania followed her.

Teresa was in the room on her own. She was happy to see her sister and embraced her. Stefania sat down. Teresa sat beside her and held her hand. She asked about everyone at home.

'You know, Stefania, one day soon I am going to ask you all to come here for *pranzo*, on a Sunday. Yes, that is what I'm going to do – is one not allowed to have family to visit? Yes, I am going to ask my husband.' She laughed when she said 'husband'.

'I am sure he will agree,' she laughed again. 'And if his mamma, papà and brothers are too high and mighty to sit at the table with us, they can go out to eat, and I hope that is what they will do so that we can enjoy ourselves.'

Stefania admired the room, and she admired Teresa, looking as if she was born in such a house. She was wearing a loose, flowing dress and her bump was already showing.

Then *la signora* Teresa rang the bell. Rosetta was summoned.

'*Si, signora*,' she said as she came in.

'Bring tea, cake and biscuits,' Teresa requested.

Stefania said, 'This is a beautiful room, you look as if you were born to it.'

'Do you want to see the rest of the house? Come, I will show you now that there is no one at home.'

Stefania was impressed by the huge empty *salone*, the dining room and the master bedroom which Teresa shared with her husband. They just put their heads through the door of Donna Beatrice's bedroom, catching a glimpse of its heavy dark furniture, many layers of curtains and huge bed. Then there were many other rooms. Teresa was excited to show her little sister the nursery. It was getting redecorated in preparation for the baby.

When downstairs, Teresa opened a dusty, dark room and went to the window to open the shutters and let some light and air in.

She said, 'They keep this room in darkness, because the sunlight makes the books fade.'

Stefania looked in awe at the many shelves of books.

'My God, how many books!'

'Yes, but no one reads them. Gian Filippo's grandfather was a lover of books, it's his collection.'

'Can I take just one away with me to read? I will

take care of it then bring it back, please Teresa… can I?'

'Go ahead, choose one, but be careful they are full of dust. I should really get the maids to clean this room, it is a disgrace!'

Stefania did not know which to take so she took one at random. She looked at the title: *I Promessi Sposi*. That would do. From then on, every time she came to visit Teresa, she would take a book. She wanted to read everything.

Gian Filippo had noticed that his sister-in-law was coming to the house more often to visit her sister. At first, she was helping the staff to clean the library. It turned out to be a massive job. They had to take all the books down, a big pile on the floor covered with dust sheets, and then the room was cleaned and a fresh coat of paint was applied. Then the three brothers set to work, cataloguing the books and putting them back on the shelves in alphabetical order. When the room was finished, it was sometimes used if not to read, at least for a quiet cup of tea.

Now when Stefania came, she would disappear into the library, take a book to read, make herself comfortable on a sofa and there she would sit all afternoon. One day Gian Filippo followed her into the study to help her to choose a book. When she had read it, he asked her if she had enjoyed it, and what her thoughts were on it. They discussed the story, and then other stories. Gian Filippo found himself enjoying the discussions he would have with her. She was a very clever girl.

Since he had married, Gian Filippo seemed years

younger. He did not look so awkward, he walked with a spring in his step. He was certainly much happier. Teresa was a girl with so much life in her. She made him laugh. There was laughter in the house now, when before there was none. He could not wait for the baby's birth; it was still five long months to wait.

At times his parents were not kind to the girl whom they thought gave herself airs and graces – after all, she was just a peasant. But he was sure that once the baby was born, they would grow to love her and put her origins behind them. They would be grateful for the new life she had brought to their dull old age.

He was debating what he could give to his young wife as a thank you for the baby. He was considering a set of matching earrings, and necklace and bracelet, maybe emeralds or diamonds. He knew that she would love them. Lately, he had been trying to think of something he could give to her now, that maybe would please her even more.

One day when Stefania came to the house Gian Filippo met her outside. She looked as if she had been crying and was flushed from the fast walk that had carried her to the house earlier than usual.

'Why have you been crying, is there something wrong at home?'

Stefania shook her head, 'No, nothing is wrong, it's just me being silly. I have been wanting something which is impossible. This morning I have decided to put all that behind me and be realistic. I have signed up for an apprenticeship with a dressmaker to learn the trade. It seems like the only thing available to me with my qualifications. What I really would love to do is become an engineer.'

Gian Filippo was surprised to hear this from a girl. An engineer!

'When do you start the dressmaking course?'

'Next week,' she said.

They went inside the house. They sat in the *piccolo salone* and Teresa rang for tea.

'I really don't like sewing, that is my problem, but its either that or I stay at home which I don't want to do, because then I will learn nothing. I think I know all there is to know about babies.'

Stefania was about to go home when Gian Filippo asked her to stay. 'In fact,' he said to her, 'go into the kitchen and tell Angelica that there will be one more for *pranzo*.' The girl did as she was told, though she would rather have been alone with Teresa.

Gian Filippo sat by his wife, kissed her hand and asked if he could feel the baby moving. It had started to do this, and it fascinated him. The baby was becoming more real to him.

'*Amore*,' he said to his wife, 'I have been thinking of something I can do to please you, because my darling you please me so much. My happiness is to see you happy.'

Teresa smiled at him, 'You are a dear, *mio caro*. I am happy right now. But what have you got in mind? You know I am always up for a surprise. Tell me.'

He said, 'Your sister is a very clever girl. She wants to be an engineer.'

Teresa laughed, 'You don't say.'

'You ask her if she wants to go to college. I will pay for it.'

Teresa looked at him, 'You would do that for me... what will your mother say?'

'It does not matter what she says.'

His wife threw her arms round his neck in gratitude. 'She will be so happy.'

Stefania came back to find them kissing. She was about to walk out again when she was called in.

'Come back, Stefania, don't go. Gian Filippo wants to talk to you.'

'No, no,' he exclaimed, 'your sister wants to talk to you.'

Teresa asked her, 'You are not happy to go to the seamstress to learn the trade, are you? It is something you don't see yourself doing for the rest of your life. I know that. Is there something else you would really like to do? What is your dream?'

Stefania wondered where this conversation was going.

'Well as I have said before, I would like to do something with my mind, rather than my hands. As you know, I love reading, learning new things, finding out how things work and solving problems. Someone once told me that I should be an engineer. Of course, I don't really know what that is, but I would like to find out.' Then she laughed, 'I am such a dreamer, but of course none of this will happen. Not for someone like me.'

Teresa responded excitedly, 'Stefania, we are going to live in Rome for the winter. Gian Filippo wants me to be where I can get good medical care, and of course he has work there. Would you like to come and live with us? Then you can go back to school and if you work hard, maybe you can have your dream come true!'

The girl could not contain her excitement; she cried big sobs. Teresa put her arms around her shoulders.

'There now, no need to cry.'

Stefania clasped her sister, 'Thank you, thank you! You have made me the happiest girl in the world.'

CHAPTER 23

Catarina

ONE OF THE tables had been moved from the kitchen. It was no longer needed, one table was enough. To see the empty places was upsetting.

Vincenzo sat at the head of the table, his father and mother to his right. At the other side was his wife, with Bruno in his highchair snug between his mother and nonna, both women ready to pop food in his mouth. Then the girls – Concettina, Stefania, Fiorinda, Annetta, Lia and Erica. Vincenzo glanced at his miracle baby, Lorenzo, who had survived a most traumatic birth. He was asleep in his crib.

After the meal was over, Vincenzo walked up the track to Colle Posta to see Giacomo. Now they had children in common, a connection, they often looked for each other to have a natter or to help each other out. Just yesterday Vincenzo had been helping him with the last of the grape harvest. The grapes were harvested as needed. He had sold most of his produce, there were just a couple of rows of vines still to be sold. Yesterday a woman from up-by, the wife of a shepherd, came and she had taken what was left. She had with her a little girl, a sweet chubby thing, and she had certainly liked her grapes.

Giacomo saw his friend coming and went back in the house. He came out with a sheet of paper in his hand. He said as he handed it to him, 'I was just about to come to your house. Here, it's a telegram from Maria.'

Vincenzo read it.

Arrived. All well. Zio well. Marco came to meet us. Letter to follow.

'What a relief. I will take this home right away.' And he left to do so.

Matilda read and reread the telegram... letter to follow. The postman was becoming her new best friend.

Catarina had come to visit – she often came now. Every time she got a letter from Francesco, she would come to tell them if there was any news. Sometimes she would make things up just to amuse them.

She would ask if they had received a letter and if they had, could she see it.

A friendship had developed between her and Concettina, and sometimes the girls would go out together, either to the market or to Picinisco for Sunday mass. Catarina sang in the church choir in Villa Latina and she had persuaded Concettina to join.

Sometimes Catarina would ask Concettina to go with her to the cinema. 'Please,' she would beg, 'come with me, I so want to go. But Francesco does not like me going. He is jealous that I might meet someone else. But if you come with me, his sister, he can't complain. Come, I will pay for you, you will be doing me a favour. They are showing a film called *Gone with the Wind*, everyone says that it is fantastic.'

Concettina went to Villa Latina for a couple of hours in the afternoon. She was going to see Filomena, a seamstress. Concettina had offered to help her without payment, so that she could learn a little of her trade. She wanted to do this so she could make clothes for her five little sisters, make them well-made clothes from scratch. She was like a second mother to the little ones, they were her family.

She had no intention to marry. She did not want to be like her mother, just over forty and already worn out between many births, hard work and worry on every level. No way, that was not for her. She had seen her mother suffer when the babies died, when the boys left – Andrea, Francesco and Osvaldo. Then Maria and the twins. And would she ever get over the death of Giovanni? Never! How she devoured that telegram and letters, she lived for them.

The girls were walking along the high road. They had stopped to speak to Adelina, who was spoon-feeding her son. He made them laugh; as soon as the soup was in his mouth, he would spit it out. Concettina, who had fed a million babies, showed Adelina how to do it. Food in, a quick distraction and then food would go down. At least it worked for two or three spoonfuls.

As the two friends walked along talking about this or that, soon they were talking about Catarina's favourite subject: Francesco. Then Catarina asked her, 'Concettina, has it ever happened to you that you have missed a monthly? I have missed two periods. I don't know why.'

Concettina looked at her in shock. Alarm bells were ringing in her head. But the look on Catarina's face was quite innocent, not at all worried. She couldn't be that clueless as to what it could be, surely not.

'No,' Concettina said. 'No, never.'

'Well, I was feeling a bit unwell, with an upset stomach. I went to the doctor and told him about it and the missed period. He said it could be stress – I was so distraught when Francesco left, I cried for weeks. He said that it would resolve itself and not to worry.' Catarina laughed. 'When I told my mother that I had been to the doctor and what he had said, she asked me some very embarrassing questions.'

Concettina waited, holding her breath. 'What did she ask you?'

'She asked me if I had... you know, done it with Francesco.'

'And?'

'No, of course not.'

'Well then, it's all right. *Tutto bene*, it will come sooner or later, not to worry,' Concettina said reassuringly before adding, 'but if you miss another period, you should ask your mother to take you to the doctor because it could be something else.'

When they arrived in Villa Latina, Catarina asked Concettina into the emporium.

'Come, I have something for you.'

Concettina did not like to go in there because she would look around and there was just too much stuff. Things that she would have loved to buy. She tried not to show her emotions to Catarina's mother and sisters.

Catarina called her mother, 'Mamma, where are all the offcuts of material we were going to get rid of?' While she said this, she winked at her mother. Her mother understood.

'They are under the stairs, ready to be thrown out.'

Catarina came back with a bundle of material. She handed them to her friend.

'Here, take them, you can make something with them now that you are learning how to sew.'

'Can I give you something for them?'

'No, no don't be silly, just take them.'

Concettina was thinking that she would bake an apple cake for her. That was just how it was in the countryside: give and take.

***

A couple of weeks passed. The family were inside. It was getting cold and the fire was lit with a good flame. Someone was outside.

'*Permesso*. Can we come in?'

'Of course, of course, come in and sit down. Concettina, get a drink or a cup of tea. See what they would like.'

From the faces of the three people seated at the table, they could see this was not a social visit. Catarina was there with her mother and father.

Her father said, 'Vincenzo, can we speak to you and your wife in private?'

Vincenzo looked around him and with his head made a movement to the rest of the family to tell them to make themselves scarce.

They were all sitting down. No one was speaking.

'Well, what is it?' asked Vincenzo.

Catarina burst into tears. Matilda's first thought was that something had happened to Francesco.

All at once, Rosina said, 'Catarina is pregnant. We have to bring Francesco back so that he can marry her.'

Vincenzo asked, 'Does Francesco know about this?'

Catarina answered, 'Yes, he knows, but he said that he is not coming back because it cannot be his child.'

Vincenzo and Matilda looked at each other in disbelief. Vincenzo said, 'Well Catarina, you should know whose child it is. If it is not Francesco's... then whose is it?'

'It must be Francesco because it cannot possibly be anyone else.'

Her father said to his daughter, 'Go outside you stupid girl.' He looked at the women sitting at the table. He said, 'Vincenzo, Matilda, the doctor said when he examined her that she is pregnant, there is no doubt about that. But she is still intact...! You know what I mean. He said that between the couple there has been serious fooling around, you know... how it is. Sometimes when there has been skin-to-skin contact, it can happen that she can conceive although there has been no penetration. And that is how we stand. Your son said that he has not had sex with her, so it can't be his child. I want you to write to Francesco, tell him what the doctor said, and to come back as soon as possible to his virgin bride.'

Vincenzo, at this point, could not help it; he had to laugh, and Matilda joined him. It was so good to hear her laugh. Before long, Catarina's parents were laughing too.

Catarina was outside crying – she couldn't believe it. What was there to laugh about?

After they had left, Vincenzo took a pen and paper to write to his son. He tried once, he tried twice. He tried a third time and again he threw the paper in the fire.

He said to Matilda, 'How do I say what I have to say in writing? This is what we will do. Tomorrow we will go to Atina, and you will bring the telephone number he has sent you. The post office has a telephone now, we will ask the postmaster to help us. We can talk to him, hear his voice, you will like that *cara*, my dear?'

She responded with, 'Yes, yes, I would like that very much.'

The following day, as they planned, they were at the post office. They were feeling nervous, agitated. They had to wait their turn before they could speak to the assistant behind the counter.

'I want to speak to my son Francesco Valente. He is in Scotland. I have his number here.'

The young man said, 'Give me the number. Sit there to wait.'

'How much will it cost?' Vincenzo asked to make sure that he had enough money.

'It's there on the list on the wall; it is fifty lira per minute for the UK.'

'That is not as much as I thought,' he said to his wife. 'We have to wait until he calls us, this person is before us.'

'Valente!' the assistant called as he showed them into the cubicle. 'See that light up there, that will tell you how much the call is going to cost you.'

He picked up the receiver and dialled some numbers. He listened. Both Vincenzo and Matilda's hearts had stopped beating.

He said, '*Signore Valente, I tuoi genitori sono qui.*' He handed the phone to Vincenzo and closed the door.

'*Papà, Papà, sei proprio tu!*'

'*Si sono io, ecco tua Mamma.*'

'*O figlio mio, figlio mio*!' – 'My darling boy, oh my dear!' was all that she could say. She passed the phone back to Vincenzo.

Vincenzo calmed down and after asking how he and his brother were, went on to talk to him man to man, explaining the situation to him, telling him to come back as soon as possible to do his duty. To fix the mess he had made.

Before bidding him goodbye, Matilda also spoke to him, just a few words, telling him how much she loved him. Then Francesco said that he would come back as soon as possible.

They paid for the telephone call – it was not that much. Matilda could not believe it. She could talk to her sons almost as if they were there standing by her side.

All of a sudden it did not feel like they were so far away. They were just there at the end of the line.

CHAPTER 24

Ten Years Later

IT WAS THE MONTH of May. The sky was dark with heavy clouds. It had rained, the trees were dripping. Tree blossoms were everywhere. The grass was sparkling with water droplets. Going up to the house, on the side of the vegetable garden, there was a row of roses in different colours, their heads drooping after the rain. Outside the house on the *terrazza* were pots and pots of geraniums.

There was a steady stream of people coming to the house; some came in cars, others walked under an umbrella which they closed and shook and left at the door before they went in. This house, which had never known silence, had fallen quiet. People talked in a hushed tone. They went quickly into the house, stayed for twenty minutes and then went home.

As you entered the large kitchen you could see that the table had been moved and, in its place, there was a coffin. At the head of the coffin, hanging on the wall, there was a dark satin cloth with tassels and a gold cross embroidered in the middle. On a stand at the side of the casket was a vase of flowers. At the foot, again there was a stand with a vase, this time filled with Holy water. The vase had a sprig of an olive tree in it. The tree of peace. The family, friends and neighbours who came to show their respect would dip the twig in the Holy water and make the sign of the cross with it on the body of the deceased. Then they would make the sign of the cross on themselves, give a small curtsy, linger for a minute, then walk over to give condolences to the weeping family who sat by the side of their loved one.

Vincenzo sat by his mother. She was in a wheelchair and already dressed in black from head to toe, black headscarf to black stockings. Her eyes were red from weeping, a bewildered look in her eyes. People came to her to hug and kiss her. They would say words to her, but in her mind it was just a murmur of voices. She would nod her head and squeeze their hand as if she had understood. Then they would move to Vincenzo and his wife, Matilda, and other members of the family.

Vincenzo's eyes were drawn to his father lying there. Where had that life gone? He would miss him so much... Andrea and Vincenzo, father and son, friend, brother. They had been everything to each other. Vincenzo knew that without the help of his father he could not have raised his brood of children, sixteen living, thanks be to God. Now he was gone at seventy-five; he still had good years in him, if the cancer had not got him. When the stream of people stopped coming, he would sit with him all night to keep his father company for one last time. Tomorrow, the funeral. First the mass in the church of San Lorenzo, then to the cemetery where Andrea had already bought a plot for himself and his wife.

Then life would go on without him... to Vincenzo, it would never be the same.

CHAPTER 25

Andrea Comes Home

ANDREA WAS WALKING down the track to his house. He was carrying a small suitcase and an open umbrella because it was raining, a gentle drizzle that reminded him of home. Home, he thought, where is home? Is it here, at this house in front of him, or was it there, that flat in a distant land which he had left in a hurry on receiving his father's letter – come quick if you can, Nonno Andrea is dying.

As he got closer to the house, he could see that the *terazza* was full of people. Mostly they were quiet, but a few spoke in a whisper. As he made his way to the front door of the house, people turned to look at him... a stranger... was he a stranger? Then he felt himself embraced by his brothers and sisters; they were all around him... so many. He found that he was crying. He was too late, Nonno Andrea had passed away.

Just then the door was opened – they were carrying the coffin outside of the house. The hearse was outside, its tail door open, ready to receive the body. His mother and father saw him and with a cry of joy ran to him.

'Oh my son, oh *figlio mio*, my darling boy,' his mother cried.

They led him to the car. Andrea stood before the coffin. He knocked on the dark wood and said, 'Nonno, I am here. I am sorry that I am too late.'

His mother held him, 'He can hear... see... you from up above, my dear.'

After three days the household returned to normal, everyone doing what had to be done. It was like that in Italy: after twenty-four hours, it was the funeral. The next few days. friends and family came to visit bringing cooked food, and that was it... all over. The man that had been a central part of that family was no more, only a memory to all who knew and loved him. God rest his soul.

Andrea was standing by the field next to the house. He could see the mare – she must be a good age by now. His father said he could not part with her, although now she was not needed, with the tractor doing most of the work around the farmstead.

Andrea went into the hayloft. There, hanging on the wall in its usual place, was the horse's harness. He walked to the gate of the field and he whistled to the horse. She stopped cropping the grass and lifted her head to look at him. He whistled again, the horse swished her tail, tossed her head and ambled towards him. 'Hello old girl,' he said as he caressed her soft, whiskered muzzle.

He led her to the barn and put on her harness. He got a rope and axe, then mounted the horse and, tugging at her reins, led her up the track to San Pietro. He let the horse go at her own pace – she knew the way. As he looked about him, he could see the mountains, he could see Picinisco, he could see everything that he remembered and had seen so many times in his head. He realised how much he had missed this place: it was home, the place of his birth. He ambled along. Every house that he passed had a memory for him, the people who lived there, the friends he went to school and grew up with.

It had been ten long years. Why had he left it so long to come back? Ten long years, why? He thought back to when he first arrived in Scotland.

When he got to Edinburgh, he worked for Tony seven days a week. Tony told him to take a day off work, but he had replied that he did not need to take a day off – he had left home to work, to get on. He saved as much as he could. A shared room above the shop was included in his wage. Occasionally, he sent something home to his parents.

When his four-year contract with Tony was over, he felt that he had saved enough for a deposit to rent a business, and that is what he did. Not long after, he heard of a fish and chip shop in Portobello, beside the sea, that was for sale, he went to see it. It was run-down and dirty, but he could see its potential at once. Yes, he had thought, this is for me. My own shop, no longer paying rent, lining someone else's pocket. He agreed to the sum he was asked, putting a payment down at once to seal the deal. He had no trouble getting a loan from the bank, and he had no trouble repaying the loan.

That was the beginning of a good relationship with the bank manager. When he bought the flat above the shop which he rented, he realised how easy it was to make money, so every time a flat came up for sale in the Portobello area he put a bid in for it. Then he bought another fish and chip shop on the promenade, next to the outdoor swimming pool. It had seating for a hundred people and in the summer it did a roaring trade.

He knew that his property was not all paid for, but he was not worried. He was making money.

That was the reason why he had not come back, he had too much to do. He certainly could not come back in the summer, but he could have come in the winter. He made a promise to himself to do that, to come to see his mother and father, not to leave it so long that he would only see them in their coffin like he had with Nonno Andrea.

Another reason why he had not come back was Agnes: he did not want to leave her and he felt that he could not ask her to come with him.

Agnes had started to work for him when she was still at school. She was a pretty girl, tall and slim, always hanging about the shop. One day he asked her if she could help him out because he was short-staffed and she jumped at the chance to work for the handsome Italian.

She was an intelligent girl and a quick learner and always available. When she left school, she became a permanent member of staff. Within a few years, one of his best workers, Agnes became his right-hand man. The girl knew more about his business than he knew himself.

On her eighteenth birthday, as a birthday treat, he took her out: they went to the pictures at the Playhouse and after for a meal at a new restaurant, The Caprice, one of the first Italian restaurants to open in Edinburgh, and on that night they became lovers.

They lived together now and he knew that she was waiting for him to marry her. To make her into an honest woman. He kept putting it off, he could not decide. She was a great girl – honest and hardworking.

In fact, he had left his business in her capable hands. He was not at all worried about his empire.

The thing that stopped him from marrying her was that she wasn't Italian. She was not like his mother or his sisters. Would he regret it in later life? Should he choose a girl to marry while he was here? He knew it would break Agnes' heart.

By this time, he had arrived at the turning to the woodland. He was going to cut some firewood, for 'old time's sake'. He was on the path and, just like old times, he could see Isabella at the well, washing clothes.

She looked up, to see who was going by.

She stood and stared at him.

'Andrea!'

He stopped, they looked at each other.

She thought that he was a *gran signore* and even more handsome. He thought, my goodness she has aged.

He was the first to speak, 'How are you, Isabella, I see you are still at the well doing the washing.'

'Yes,' she said, 'not much has changed here. You are looking well, still *un bel giovane*, still handsome.' She smiled at him… for old time's sake.

'I see Antonio, as usual, is not around. Is he keeping well?' he returned her smile.

He noticed that she kept looking over his shoulder, in the distance. He looked that way.

'That is my son, he is coming back from school.'

'What is his name?' he asked.

'His name is Raffaele, we called him after Antonio's father.'

'Is he your only child?'

'Yes,' she said.

'How old is he?'

She looked away and he could see that she was not comfortable with him asking so many questions.

'He is nine years old.' She glanced to the side, she did not want to meet his eyes.

As the boy came closer, he could not take his eyes off him. There was no doubt! The boy looked just like his father and brothers.

I want my children to look like that – Italian, he thought. If he married Agnes, his children would have red hair and freckles – his mother, his grandparents would be Scottish. He had great respect for the Scottish people. They had given him so much, but this feeling he had was bigger than him, he could not help it.

As he slowly made his way home with the horse behind him, Andrea was deep in thought. The boy, Raffaele – there was no doubt in his mind that he was his son, and from the look on Isabella's face she knew it too. She could not look in his eyes.

He was sure that if he said anything to her, if he asked her if he was his son, she would fiercely deny it – how dare he say such a thing, he was Antonio's son. He was named after Antonio's father, Raffaele.

Andrea thought back to their brief affair. At the time, his blood was up, he could not resist her. But now, in a calmer frame of mind, he could see that perhaps it was she who had seduced him for motives of her own.

Then his thoughts went to Agnes, his sweet Agnes waiting for him, counting the days until his return. Just the thought of her gave him a longing to go home to her. He missed her, he loved her. This separation from her had done him good: it had blown away all the indecision he had about marrying her. He could not imagine being with anyone else.

Yes, he wanted to go home. It was nice to be here, and from now on he would come more often and bring Agnes with him to meet his folk. But his life was there with Agnes in his new home and country, Scotland.

CHAPTER 26

Back from America

CONCETTINA WAS IN the back room. The ground floor of the house, which had been used for storing fuel for the fire, hay and other foodstuff for them and the animals, had been converted back to a living space. One of the rooms was now Nonna Concetta's bedroom. There was a bathroom next to the bedroom and another bathroom upstairs... two bathrooms, what luxury! Before, they had only an outside toilet. Concettina was helping her grandmother get out of bed, carefully putting the wheelchair next to the bed. She then wheeled her to the bathroom to get her washed and dressed.

It was a beautiful sunny day. 'Do you want to go outside, Nonna? It's nice and warm in the sunshine. Yes, go. See, Mamma is already there. I will bring you a cappuccino just as you like it, nice and hot, and a piece of apple cake.' She wheeled her out then went to make the coffee.

Matilda could see that the old woman was looking a little confused since the death of her husband. '*Buongiorno* Mamma, how are you feeling this morning? I know you are missing Papà Andrea, we all are... come here, look at the flowers, they are so beautiful. But they are so dry, here is the hose – give them a good drink.'

She placed the hose in the old woman's hand. 'The roses too, I just love roses, they are my favourite. Do you remember, Mamma, just ten years ago we could not permit ourselves even a single flower? We had to save our resources, not waste money to buy flowers, or waste water to water them, or waste time looking after them when you could be doing something useful? I know you are still so careful about everything. I must thank you for that, and that bit of pension that you and Papà Andrea received helped us out of a hole many times.'

Concettina came out with the cappuccino and cake. 'Nonna, come to the table to drink your coffee.'

Matilda pushed the chair to the table. All three sat there to enjoy the early sunshine.

Matilda looked at Concettina. She could not understand her; her eldest daughter was now thirty years old and still at home. She was not happy about that, she would like to see her doing something with her life, having children of her own instead of staying at home to be a second mother to her brothers and sisters. When she was younger, she had had offers of marriage and even now an older bachelor or a widower with children would seek her out and propose to her. She would laugh in their faces, 'I am fine as I am, I do not need any of that... thank you.' And she was happy; nothing would have been worse for Matilda than to see her daughter unhappy.

Matilda could see her mother in the vegetable garden. She would get up at dawn to go there to set the seeds in trays, transplant them in rows and rows of weed-free, well-manured earth. She had everything growing there now that there was plenty of water. The well had an electric pump, so there was no need to draw the water by hand with the bucket. The water came out the end of a hose ready to water the plants.

Matilda knew that her mother was growing more than they needed: she was preparing for a visit. Her son was coming. Her son whom she had not seen for twenty years, Alfonso. He was coming with his wife and two sons, Antonio and Giuseppe. He was coming from America. They had already prepared the two rooms at the back for them. Matilda was so glad they had made one of the rooms smaller to make space for a bathroom. When Matilda thought of Alfonso's sons, Antonio and Giuseppe, her heart would jump and miss a beat – she did not know how she would cope with seeing them again, and not as her own.

Maria and her husband Marco were also coming with their three children, grandchildren she would meet for the first time. To see Maria again, what joy! Her daughter and family would stay with Giacomo as Marco wanted to be with his family, but she was sure that she would see them every day. She got up to help her mother in the vegetable garden where they would talk over the coming event. Fourteen more days. They were counting.

Matilda went back into the house to get the midday meal ready. She thought about what she would make. Something quick and easy; after all, they would have their main meal in the evening. Matilda would have an espresso ready for Vincenzo when he was back from work at six o'clock and they would sit at the table under the fig tree and talk for a while before he worked on the farm for a couple of hours. They would eat at eight o'clock. However, eight o'clock was too late for the grandmothers – they would complain that the food would lie in their stomachs all night, so they ate at six o'clock, something made just for them or whatever she had cooked in advance for the family meal.

The midday meal was very troublesome: the nonnas wanted pasta because they were so used to having pasta every day, the girls wanted a *panino* with mortadella, the boys wanted sausage or fried egg with *patatine* and Concettina wanted salad because she said she was getting fat. It was hard to keep everyone happy. Matilda remembered how, just ten years ago, all the family ate what there was and never complained. She was glad she had Concettina to help. At other times, Concettina would make pasta for everyone and insist that was their meal. 'EAT OR GO HUNGRY' and they ate what was put in front of them. There was no argument, there was no reasoning with her once she had said that was it.

The food was ready, they were just waiting for the children to come home from school. It would be half past one before they arrived. Bruno and Lorenzo went to the primary school in Villa Latina; they walked home. Lia and Erica went to secondary school in Atina; they came home by bus. Once everyone was home, the house came to life. It was not always happy: there were many arguments between them and sometimes they were very rude and disobedient to herself and even to the grandmothers. The only one they would not dare to be cheeky to was Concettina – she ruled with an iron fist. Sometimes she wondered how the children would permit themselves to be so disrespectful to adults. Her other children (the big ones) would not have dared. She blamed that thing there, that square box sitting on the sideboard. No good came from it. The children had begged and begged their father, 'Everyone has one!' they had cried. Vincenzo had felt as if he had no choice, he had to buy a television, or he would never get any peace.

It was eight o'clock before the family were sitting at the table eating dinner, all heads turned towards the television. Even Nonna Maria and Nonna Concetta, who sat to the side because they had already eaten, were listening, engrossed.

Vincenzo sat at the head of the table. His father's chair lay empty, no one had the courage to sit on it. He had asked his mother to move up, to sit beside him and she had just shaken her head, she needed time. On his left, his wife and Concettina, then Fiorinda and Annetta who had just returned home; they worked in Cassino training to be nurses. At the end of the table were the little ones, Lia, Erica, Bruno and Lorenzo. All heads turned to that damn television. All conversation, all interaction they had before that contraption came into the house, all gone.

Vincenzo thought back over the last ten years. So much had changed. The biggest change of all was when Pietro bought the tractor. Whoever had invented the tractor deserved a medal – it was such a useful tool to make the lives of so many people better. The tractor made easy work of many things about the farm; what had taken days of back-breaking work could now be done in an hour, and done better too. Whoever invented that blasted television deserved to be shot, or so he thought, which he was sure was not the opinion of many others, including his children.

The tractor had left him with so much spare time. When Pietro told him that there was a job going at the soap factory as a caretaker, he jumped at the chance. Since then, he had never looked back. Every month a wage. Money! They could spend some and save some for a rainy day, but only a tiny amount because now every child and every woman wanted this, that and everything. Sometimes, he thought that they were better off when they just had enough to eat, somewhere warm to sleep and friends to play with. It was enough then; now, it was never enough.

Finally, the day arrived. Giacomo and Vincenzo each hired a car to go to the Port of Naples and bring their children home. What joy, what happiness, to see them again and to see grandchildren whom they had never met. Vincenzo recalled the day he had brought Maria, Antonio and Giuseppe to the Port to wave goodbye to them as the massive ship pulled away across the great ocean. He had felt like a horse had kicked him in the stomach. There must be few other occasions more painful to a parent than to see their child disappearing, not knowing if you would ever see them again.

They stood at the pier waiting for them to disembark, and there they soon were, walking down the gangway. Vincenzo recognised Maria right away. The men were both waving, 'We are here, we are here!'

Maria was the first to see them. She let go of her case and ran into her father's arms. The rest of the group stood back and looked; they were strangers to each other. Marco went to his father; they had not seen each other for twenty years. Both were thinking, how he has aged, and they embraced, both in tears.

Vincenzo could not take his eyes off the two young

men. Two beautiful boys, still like two peas in a pod, but now they looked like his father, their grandfather Andrea. It was uncanny how much they resembled him. They came to him, to greet him, a hand outstretched with a 'hello Zio'. He had no words, he could not speak. He tried to act as normal as possible, but these two words had broken his heart.

At home, they all waited. At last, the two cars were coming down the track in a cloud of dust. The mothers held on to each other in anticipation. Matilda supported her mother. She could feel her trembling – it had been twenty long years since she had seen her son.

She went to him, 'Alfonso, Alfonso, *figlio mio*.'

Maria, Antonio and Giuseppe ran to their mother to embrace her. Vincenzo went to them too, he wanted to be with them. The boys were crying now, saying, 'Mamma, Papà, we have missed you so much. We know that you did it for our good. We are happy. Thank you for your sacrifice.' They turned to include Alfonso and his wife in the group.

Matilda embraced her brother and whispered, 'Thank you, brother.'

CHAPTER 27

Family Reunion

'COME, GIRLS, HELP me take these tables outside,' said Matilda and, to the rest of the family, 'Pietro, Francesco, go into the barn, bring out the other old table and any others you can find.

'Bruno, Lorenzo, Lia, Erica, find all the chairs and stools that are in the house, and take them outside.

'Vincenzo, are you keeping an eye on the lamb? Make sure that there is always someone there turning the spit.

'Mamma, can you go to the *orto* and pick all the salad stuff? Annetta, you go to help Nonna.

'Mamma Concetta, how are you doing shelling the peas? Do get the children to help you.

'Vincenzo, is the bread baked? Can you take it out so that we can put the food in to cook?

'Concettina, can you keep these children under control?'

At last, all was ready: the table set under the fig tree, the food cooked.

Vincenzo and Matilda were taking a well-deserved rest.

Nonna Maria and Nonna Concetta sat side by side. They were surveying the scene. Out of respect for Nonno Andrea, there was no music.

They could see Teresa, Gian Filippo and their son, Stefano, arriving in the car.

Marco and Maria were walking down the track.
Osvaldo was getting out of his car, making sure that his tunic was looking good on him.
Francesco and Catarina had already arrived, bringing trays of sweet cakes from the *pasticceria*, bakery.
Pietro and his family had been helping since morning.
Andrea, again his father's right-hand man, helped him butcher the lamb and was now helping at the oven.
The only one who was not coming was Stefania. She had just been taken on by a top engineering firm in Milan and she could not get away.
They were all there, the children and the grandchildren. To have them all together... what joy.

Afterword

THIS WORK OF fiction, like my other books, it is set in the town of Picinisco in Lazio, Italy. I got my inspiration from a headstone in the cemetery there. It bore only these words:

AN EXEMPLARY MOTHER OF NINETEEN CHILDREN.

Children of this Land unfolds during the 1950s when the people of southern Lazio were recovering from the Second World War. The Valentes are a large family who made their living, like so many others at that time, by working the land. Families of eight to ten children were common and it was a struggle to support them. It took sheer strength and determination, and making the most of what little they had. Most families did not own their own land, so they had to give half of whatever they produced to the landlord.

Many fled all over the world, leaving a void in the hearts of those they left behind.

The farmers who worked the land had a hard life, but they did not go hungry as there was always plenty food; the folk that lived in the towns were not so lucky. Although poor, these farmers were by no means unhappy and this story has many joyful events. They were poor, but not miserable.

The small town of Picinisco sits at an altitude of 800

metres in the foothills of the Abruzzi National Park. My first book, *The Wee Italian Girl*, is autobiographical: my story as a child at eight years of age. I recall my last year of living in a small village in the mountains of Picinisco, bringing to life the people and their way of life. My father was a shepherd, and we moved between our home in the mountains in the summer and the low valleys when the snow came… then we left it all behind and emigrated to Scotland.

My second book, *Domenica: A Girl from Montecassino*, is again based on a true story, this time that of my husband's family. Forced to leave their home in the mountains by the threat of war, they travelled to a 'safer' place where calamity befell their family of nine. Only six returned to their devastated mountain home and Domenica, the eldest, was only sixteen. It is the story of their survival and the consequences of war on one family.

Picinisco is a beautiful mountain town with many more stories to tell, and in reading all three books, I hope you will get to know and love Picinisco more and more… and maybe want to visit. Many people left and emigrated all over the world, returning with stories of their new homes far away. But a love for Picinisco as deep as the valleys and as pure as the snow-capped mountains is never forgotten.

Serafina Crolla

Luath Press Limited

committed to publishing well written books worth reading

LUATH PRESS takes its name from Robert Burns, whose little collie Luath (*Gael.*, swift or nimble) tripped up Jean Armour at a wedding and gave him the chance to speak to the woman who was to be his wife and the abiding love of his life. Burns called one of the 'Twa Dogs' Luath after Cuchullin's hunting dog in Ossian's *Fingal*. Luath Press was established in 1981 in the heart of Burns country, and is now based a few steps up the road from Burns' first lodgings on Edinburgh's Royal Mile. Luath offers you distinctive writing with a hint of unexpected pleasures.

Most bookshops in the UK, the US, Canada, Australia, New Zealand and parts of Europe, either carry our books in stock or can order them for you. To order direct from us, please send a £sterling cheque, postal order, international money order or your credit card details (number, address of cardholder and expiry date) to us at the address below. Please add post and packing as follows: UK – £1.00 per delivery address; overseas surface mail – £2.50 per delivery address; overseas airmail – £3.50 for the first book to each delivery address, plus £1.00 for each additional book by airmail to the same address. If your order is a gift, we will happily enclose your card or message at no extra charge.

ILLUSTRATION: IAN KELLAS

Luath Press Limited
543/2 Castlehill
The Royal Mile
Edinburgh EH1 2ND
Scotland
Telephone: 0131 225 4326 (24 hours)
Email: sales@luath.co.uk
Website: www.luath.co.uk